"You can't expect me to make a decision this quickly."

"That's all right," Massimo said. "I've been single for thirty-four years. Nicky and I can wait one more day to learn our fate."

"One more day—" Julie cried in frustration.

"In case you need reminding, I hired you to be Nicky's nanny within a half hour of your tearful petition."

Even if what he'd said was blatantly true, the man didn't play fair with her emotions. "A nanny's quite different from a wife."

"In title only," he answered in a mild tone. "Nothing has to change for us privately."

Her face went hot. "I can promise you it won't!"

"Then I have my answer. Shall we put it in writing?"

Her expression turned mutinous. "I haven't agreed to anything yet."

"That's where you're wrong," he whispered.

Harlequin Romance®

is thrilled to bring you an exciting
new book from fan-favorite author

REBECCA WINTERS

Wonderfully unique every time,
Rebecca Winters will take you on an
emotional roller coaster! Her powerful
stories will enthrall your senses and leave
you on a romantic high....

"Rebecca Winters...is pure magic."
—*Romantic Times BOOKreviews*

REBECCA WINTERS

The Italian Tycoon and the Nanny

MEDITERRANEAN DADS

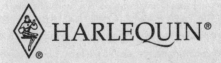

HARLEQUIN®

TORONTO • NEW YORK • LONDON
AMSTERDAM • PARIS • SYDNEY • HAMBURG
STOCKHOLM • ATHENS • TOKYO • MILAN • MADRID
PRAGUE • WARSAW • BUDAPEST • AUCKLAND

ISBN-13: 978-0-373-17500-0
ISBN-10:   0-373-17500-0

THE ITALIAN TYCOON AND THE NANNY

First North American Publication 2008.

This edition published by arrangement with Harlequin Books S.A.

® and TM are trademarks of the publisher. Trademarks indicated with ® are registered in the United States Patent and Trademark Office, the Canadian Trade Marks Office and in other countries.

www.eHarlequin.com

Printed in U.S.A.

MEDITERRANEAN DADS

These billionaires swap bachelorhood for fatherhood!

Meet Massimo Rinaldi di Rocche and Cesar Villon de Falcon

Best friends, Massimo and Cesar are known to the world as billionaire bachelors who drink the finest French champagne, wear the most luxurious Italian suits and party with the A-list celebrity crowd in Monaco.

But, Mediterranean to their core, they also believe in tradition, honor and always putting family first!

In May—
The Italian Playboy's Secret Son

Race-car driver and Monaco's most notorious playboy Cesar finds out his one night of passion with childhood sweetheart Sarah had consequences he never imagined....

Rebecca Winters, whose family of four children has now swelled to include three beautiful grandchildren, lives in Salt Lake City, Utah, in the land of the Rocky Mountains. With canyons and high alpine meadows full of wildflowers, she never runs out of places to explore. They, plus her favorite vacation spots in Europe, often end up as backgrounds for her Harlequin Romance® novels. Writing is her passion, along with her family and church. Rebecca loves to hear from her readers. If you wish to e-mail her, please visit her Web site at www.cleanromances.com.

Rebecca Winters on
The Italian Tycoon and the Nanny
"Is there anything greater than a lovable woman, a noble man and a precious baby, all coming together under unusual circumstances to give us the hope and promise of a happier tomorrow? I don't think so."

CHAPTER ONE

THE phone in Massimo's pocket rang, but this time he didn't answer it. What part of no didn't Gillian Pittman understand? She was the only female professor in the group and could have her pick of a dozen men. But she'd set her sights on Massimo, and he didn't return the compliment.

When he wanted feminine companionship, he spent the odd weekend in Mexico City or Positano with his favorite person, Cesar, who happened to be reigning champion of the Grand Prix. His second cousin's addiction to racing ensured plenty of women for both of them.

After a grueling workday, he craved a tall glass of ice water followed by a long hot and cold running shower that operated at maximum pressure. Too bad no such luxuries awaited him in the tent he'd called home for the past two years.

It was no bigger than a large, airless closet. Set in the heart of the Petén forest of Guatemala, it offered little more than a place to eat, sleep and record his findings.

The professional teams working at the Cancuen dig site lived in a compound on the other side of the Mayan palace they were excavating. It offered a few more amenities. But he'd come here on his own in an unofficial capacity. To join them after hours meant sacrificing his privacy, something he wasn't prepared to do.

As he undid the lid on a bottle of water, his phone beeped. Irritated by the intrusion, he drained the contents before checking to see what was so important Dr. Pittman had resorted to sending him a text message. But a quick glance revealed it was Sansone who'd been trying to reach him.

An ominous presentiment stole through his body.

In the twenty-four months he'd been gone, he'd never received a phone call from his oldest cousin, let alone a text message. Sansone disliked him too intensely for that.

Steeling himself to deal with it, he pushed the button and read, *Tragic news, Massimo. Call me immediately.*

The word *tragic* had a specific connotation he couldn't in all conscience ignore. Had his uncle been injured? Or worse?

In that moment before he called his cousin back, the sweat poured off him faster than when he was subjected to the sun's full intensity.

"What's happened?" he asked, the second he heard Sansone's voice.

"Papa had news that caused him to collapse. The doctor's with him, so he asked me to phone you."

He wouldn't put it past his uncle Aldo to pretend he was ill to gain Massimo's sympathy. This could be a manipulative ploy on his uncle's part to get him to come home.

Massimo wasn't ready to do that. Something earthshaking would have to happen first.

"What news might that be?"

After an uncharacteristic hesitation he said, "It's about Pietra."

With the mention of Massimo's sister, the air froze in his lungs. "What about her?"

"Her father-in-law called to tell Papa that she and his son were killed in a car accident earlier today."

Killed—

Pietra?

He reeled. Breathtaking pain shot through him.

"And the baby?" he demanded savagely.

"I don't know. Papa didn—"

Massimo hung up, unwilling for Sansone to hear any part of his grief.

"I'm afraid I have to be in Portland tomorrow for the beginning of that three-day conference, Julie. Let me know the day and time of the funeral. I'll try to arrange a flight from there."

When Brent sounded preoccupied, it meant he was sitting in front of his computer doing work. Somehow Julie had expected more from the man who professed to love her.

She gripped the phone tighter, too overwrought with grief to think clearly. Shawn's death hadn't fully sunk in yet.

While her heart ached for her helpless, orphaned nephew, she was still mourning the brother she'd loved. She couldn't believe Pietra, her charming sister-in-law, was gone. The loss was agonizing enough without trying to process the horror of the crash that had snatched two precious lives from existence.

"I wish I could tell you something definitive, but we're waiting for Pietra's uncle to phone back. Until he does, nothing can be settled," she whispered in an unsteady voice. "When I think of Nicky…"

"The little guy won't remember any of this. Luckily he's got your mom."

She bit her bottom lip so hard she tasted blood. "As I told

you yesterday after hearing the news, Nicky has *me*, Brent. My mother has already been a mother."

He made a strange sound in his throat. "Except that you work in San Francisco. How are you going to do that and take care of a baby, too?"

The answer seemed obvious to Julie. Yet by his posing that question, her hope that he wanted a future with her under any and all circumstances died on the spot.

"I…I'm planning to move here to Sonoma." Since learning of the fatal accident from her father, the idea had been growing in her mind. She intended to phone her boss and resign before the day was out.

"And give up the great job I helped you get in order to tend a child that's not even yours?"

Oh, Brent.

She shook her head. Why did it have to take a tragedy like this for her to see just how self-absorbed he was? They would never have made it. He wasn't ready for marriage, let alone interested in helping her raise Shawn's boy.

"What's the matter now?"

Now?

She guessed a lot was the matter. In retrospect it had been for a long time. But she'd let certain issues slide in the hope that things would get better.

"Why aren't you talking to me? Julie?"

He really didn't understand.

"My nephew just lost his parents. It's all I can think about right now."

"Why do you have to be the one to sacrifice everything?"

"Because I want to!"

Her emotional cry must have gotten through to him because there was a long silence.

Clearly he couldn't meet her expectations. Brent didn't have the maturity or the desire. How could she have thought he was the right man for her? Where was her judgment?

"So what are you saying?" he finally said.

She took a deep breath. "I guess I'm saying goodbye. I had some wonderful times with you, but it's over, Brent. It has to be. I think we've both known it for a while." She hung up.

Her mind on Nicky, Julie left the master bedroom and rushed into the nursery where she'd slept on the twin bed last night. He hadn't moved since she'd given him his last bottle. After he'd put up such a struggle, it was no wonder.

He didn't know her!

Four weekend visits in five months weren't enough for him to reach for her. She wasn't his mommy.

Last evening and during the night he'd fought the formula Pietra kept on hand for a supplement to her breast-feeding. Julie had rummaged in the cupboards to look for it. But he wasn't having any of it. He wanted his mother and had been inconsolable.

Today he'd finally stopped rooting long enough to take the bottle and drain it, almost as if he realized his life had changed and he was resigned to his fate.

It killed Julie inside.

She looked down at him, studying his fine blond hair and facial features. Shawn's contribution. Pietra had bequeathed him her olive complexion and dark eyes.

But his sturdy, long-limbed body didn't appear to belong to either of them. Nicky had weighed in at nine pounds three ounces, too big a baby for his small-framed mother. Julie had a feeling he was going to be a lot taller than her five-ten brother.

"Where did that mouth come from?" she whispered, tracing the outline with her finger. Just once on her last visit she'd coaxed a fleeting smile from him. It was wider than his parents'. He would break hearts one day.

He had already broken hers, but he didn't know that yet. Who could guess how long he would try to push her away while he waited for his parents to reappear?

How much did a five-month-old understand about the fact that they were gone and would never come home again? A sob escaped her throat. Probably a lot more than mere mortals could comprehend.

She had no doubt that Nicky was missing the sweet smell of his mother's skin—the way she held and loved him—the touching way she called him Niccolo.

Pietra had supplied his first nourishment upon entering the world, tendered by words rushing from her soul as she whispered her joy to him. Hers was the familiar voice he'd listened to while he'd been in her womb waiting to be born.

Fresh tears welled behind Julie's swollen eyelids.

Who would be able to comfort him when he didn't hear his father's laughter, or feel him blow on his tummy after a diaper change? Whose strong arms would never again carry him with fatherly pride, arms that had held him minutes after he was born, letting him know he was adored.

In a matter of seconds the security of that loving haven had been wiped out forever by a drunk driver. In its place…chaos.

One more kiss to the baby's forehead followed by salty tears and Julie slipped out of the nursery to go downstairs. But strident voices coming from the living room caused her to pause on the landing.

"Lem has an important court case coming up and needs to get back to Honolulu soon, so a big funeral is out. We'll have a graveside service for them here. Father Meersman has agreed to officiate. It's all I can handle."

"We have to wait for Pietra's uncle to call us back, Margaret. Despite the problems, he *did* raise her and her brother after their parents were killed. He has equal input in any decisions."

"As far as I'm concerned, after ignoring her because she married my son, he has no rights."

"Shawn was my son, too," he reminded her in a quiet voice. "He would expect us to do the decent thing for Pietra. For our daughter-in-law's sake I'll have to insist we wait for him, Margaret."

"Don't use that patriarchal tone with me, Frank."

"I'll do whatever's necessary in order to make certain the right thing is done here. No doubt her uncle has been thrust into considerable pain from the shock. That's why the doctor's with him. In case this news has softened him, their deaths might have achieved something that couldn't be accomplished in life."

"Spoken by the paragon of virtue."

Julie winced to hear her mother's bitterness come out. Her parents had been divorced ten years. Both had eventually remarried and moved from Sonoma. Yet by the way they were reacting, it could have been yesterday.

Her mother had always been difficult. There was probably a medical name for it. Julie noticed their respective spouses had absented themselves from Shawn's house. With good reason.

"Margaret—we'll have to put our personal differences aside and consider what's best for Nicky."

"Funny how you didn't worry about Julie and Shawn when you walked out. But for that, Shawn might sti—"

"Don't go there, Mom. Dad's right," Julie cried, entering the room, hating the resurrected pain that never really went away. As usual when her parents were together on the rare occasion, her mother managed to turn the conversation ugly.

Their heads swiveled in her direction. In the past twenty-four hours they'd aged. So had she.

"Nicky didn't ask for any of this. We need to concentrate on what's going to happen to *him*. He's all alone and sick! Except for the babysitter, he's among virtual strangers!"

Her mother's cheeks filled with angry color. "That's my point, Julie. Surely you don't think we need the input of a tyrant who terrified Pietra so much she married our son in order to get away from him—"

"He's still her flesh and blood. She never made him out to be a tyrant. An autocrat maybe." Julie didn't understand all the feelings that went into their complicated relationship.

"Is there a distinction?" she lashed out.

Her mother's misplaced anger was transparent.

"Lest you forget, Margaret, our son and Pietra fell in love."

"I wasn't born yesterday. Pietra made certain she got pregnant. She planned her seduction very carefully so Shawn would have no choice but to marry her and bring her to the States. Well, he did that. Now look what's happened!"

And you never forgave her for it.

Pietra *had* come between Shawn and their possessive mother, but love had been the culprit. Nothing else.

Her mother's head reared. "Julie? You'll have to come to Hawaii with us. I certainly can't raise a child all over again by myself. Lem will give you a part-time job so—"

Julie didn't hear the rest because the house phone rang. She hoped it was the pediatrician.

"I'll get it." She ran into the kitchen and clicked on. "Hello?"

"Ms. Marchant?"

"Yes?"

"This is Katy at Dr. Barlow's office. He says to change the baby the second he's wet, then put on the cream he's prescribed. I'll call it in to our clinic pharmacy right now. If the redness doesn't start to go away soon, you're to phone us."

"Thank you. He was so miserable all night."

"It should clear it up."

"What's the address?"

After learning it, she hung up and ran back in the living room. "Dad? That was the doctor. Would you mind running by the pharmacy? It's on Center Street and Wolcott. Dr. Barlow ordered a special cream for Nicky."

"I'll go right now."

He gave her a hug before walking out the door. She was glad he'd left them alone. The time had come to deal with her mother. Love for Nicky had reinforced her spine.

Once her father was gone she said, "I'm not going to Hawaii, Mom. Actually I was hoping to use any money from Shawn's insurance policy so I can stay in the town house and look after Nicky."

"If you think you can move in here with your latest boyfriend, then you c—"

"No," she cut her off. Anything but. "I won't be seeing him anymore."

"When did this transpire?"

Julie could tell her mother was pleased by the news. She'd lost Shawn to marriage, and didn't want to lose her daughter the same way.

"It doesn't matter. The fact is, I want to take care of Nicky."

"We'll do it together, Julie."

All her life Julie's mother had expected the world to revolve around her. Over the years the demands she'd placed on their family had driven a wedge. First their father had left.

Then Shawn, who did the unspeakable by marrying without her consent. Julie moved to San Francisco after college.

Her gaze flew around the front room of the small, Spanish-style town house. Shawn and Pietra had made a happy home in Sonoma where he worked for a winery.

Everywhere she looked, from pictures to baby toys and quilts, evidence of Nicky's angelic presence in the house surrounded them.

"Aside from the fact that it wouldn't be fair to Lem, *this* is Nicky's home," she reasoned quietly.

Her mother's eyes glittered. "Not anymore."

Her mother seemed beyond reason, but Julie had to try. "Pietra loved Sonoma because it reminded her of Italy where she met Shawn and they fell in love. They planned a life here with Nicky. We can't take that away from him. He's lost everything else."

"Any insurance money will be put in a fund for Nicky's college. Your father and I are in agreement there."

"In that case I'll find a way to work at home so I can stay here with him."

"Have you forgotten I'm his grandmother?"

"You just admitted you can't do it alone. I'm his aunt, and I'm the right age to do it alone," she declared.

Her mother gestured impatiently. "You're only twenty-four. You don't know the first thing about being a mother."

No, Julie didn't. In fact, she was terrified of doing everything wrong, or worse, not knowing what to do at all. But that was beside the point.

"Did you and dad know how to be parents when you first brought Shawn home from the hospital?"

Having caught her mother off guard, she took advantage of the silence. "I was on the phone to the baby's doctor before you and Lem got here. Nicky finally took a whole bottle a little while ago. I'll learn as I go. It'll work."

"It's not going to happen, Julie. You might as well know the truth now."

"What truth?" Her mother had been working up to something.

"Lem is filing papers with the court to give me custody of Nicky. That's why I've planned to have graveside services the day after tomorrow, then fly right on to Hawaii with him. I want you with us. It's a necessary precaution in case Pietra's uncle gets any funny ideas."

Julie frowned. "About what?"

"About wanting to claim his niece's male child now that Shawn isn't alive. You know how possessive Italian men are."

"Not really."

Italians didn't have the monopoly on that particular trait. Julie's mother was a case in point. This was simply another ploy on her part to manipulate Julie, but she wasn't buying it. Not this time.

"You look tired, Mom. Why don't you lie down while I check on Nicky."

"If he's awake, bring him down, will you please? I want to feed him."

For the moment, her parent was through talking. Julie went back upstairs to the nursery, her thoughts on her mother's comment. In truth she had no idea what Italian men were like. She'd seen some pictures of Pietra's family, but she'd never met any of them. From what she gathered they were a pretty formidable bunch.

According to Shawn, the Di Rocche empire had a reputation for being among the wealthiest and most influential of all the old Milanese families in Italy.

Until his untimely death, Pietra's father, Ernesto, had worked alongside his older brother, Aldo. From that point on, Aldo had raised her and her brother along with his own three sons. Today Aldo Di Rocche stood as the powerful head of the consortium which included a vast number of banking and commercial interests.

Strictly by chance Shawn had met Pietra at one of the Di Rocche vineyards. One thing led to another and they fell in love. Shawn married Pietra in secret, then told everyone after the fact. It was a brilliant move. Neither her uncle nor their mother could do anything about it.

Julie had applauded their decision. Especially when she'd learned about the tension Pietra had lived with growing up in a household with an authoritarian uncle and three male cousins who had little use for her.

The only person Pietra felt close to was her older brother whom she loved, but he lived in another part of the world. Julie could understand why. Whether families were torn apart by divorce or death, the consequences were life changing.

She stared down at the baby. Was it possible her mother was right and Pietra's uncle would try to get custody? He had the money and the clout, but Julie couldn't bear the thought of it.

Her fingers curled around the bars of the crib. "Let's hope your grandmother's wrong. You want to stay here with me, don't you, sweetheart? I love you so much."

He was still asleep on his back, his arms outstretched at either side of his head, his hands closed into semifists. While she stood there fighting more tears, her father came into the room. He handed her the sack from the pharmacy.

She quickly changed Nicky's diaper, applying the cream to his little backside that was bright red.

"You're going to make a wonderful mother someday," he murmured.

"Thanks, Dad." When her mother went back to the hotel, Julie would tell her father her plans. He'd be on her side.

She wrapped a fussing Nicky in a receiving blanket and picked him up, giving him a kiss on both cheeks. As she started out of the room, her father called her back.

"There's something I need to tell you before we go downstairs. It's going to kill your mother."

Alarm caused the hairs to prickle on the back of her neck. "D-did you hear from Pietra's uncle?"

"No. He's too ill to come, but her brother, Massimo, has arrived. He checked in at MacArthur Place. I just got off the phone with him from the mortuary. He was able to give me more information about Pietra to put in the obituary.

"Honey—" He cleared his throat. "Did you know Shawn and Pietra made out a will?"

She blinked. "No, but most couples have one."

"It's natural of course, but apparently they appointed him the baby's guardian should anything to happen to them."

What?

Pain stabbed at her heart, causing her to gasp. She stared at her father. "I don't understand—he's a bachelor who lives and works in a primitive area of the world. He's never even seen Nicky!" She couldn't understand why he'd never even been to see the baby.

Her dad's features looked gaunt. "Nevertheless that was their wish. He came for a quick visit before Nicky was born. They talked it over then."

Few things in life had hurt Julie more than this.

"He gave me the name of Shawn's attorney. I called him on the way home from the pharmacy. Your mother and I were named beneficiaries of Shawn's estate and insurance money, but Nicky goes with Pietra's brother.

"The will's iron clad. Your mother can plague Lem till the cows come home, but for all his legal expertise he won't be able to break it."

Devastated by the news, Julie nestled the baby closer. "W-what are her brother's intentions?" she whispered. "Did he tell you anything?"

A heavy sigh escaped. "He's coming over here later to see Nicky and talk to us. As far as the funeral goes, he doesn't want to interfere with any plans we've made. But after it's over, he'll be taking the baby back with him."

"Back where?" Her voice shook. "The man spends his life hacking his way through jungles in Central America!"

"I'm as stunned by this as you are."

Her father looked wounded. Julie wasn't the only one hurt by this news.

After learning about the accident, she hadn't thought anything could bring her spirits lower. But this revelation had torn the heart right out of her body. She had to do something before it was too late.

Her mother's remarks still rang in her ears.

I'm going to get custody of Nicky in case Pietra's uncle gets any funny ideas about wanting to claim his niece's male child now that Shawn isn't alive. You know how possessive Italian men are.

"Dad—don't tell mother about the will yet. She wants to feed Nicky. While she does that, I need to run to the store for a minute." A white lie could be forgiven. "When I get back, we'll talk to her together."

"That's a good idea. I need some time to collect my thoughts first. Come to your grandpa." He reached for the baby who refused to be comforted. "Let's go warm a bottle, shall we?"

After finding her purse, Julie followed her father downstairs. Relieved to discover her mother was either in the kitchen or the bathroom, she slipped out the front door to the driveway.

At four in the afternoon the temperature had climbed into the nineties. Coupled with August's moderate humidity, the interior of her car was hot to the touch. She started up the air-conditioning and headed for the luxury hotel near Sonoma Plaza.

En route she practiced what she was going to say to Pietra's brother if she could find him. Nothing sounded right. By the time she'd reached her destination and had approached the front desk, she was a mass of nerves.

"I'm here to see Mr. Massimo Di Rocche. Would you ring his room, please?"

"Certainly. Your name?"

"Julie Marchant."

After a full minute the clerk gave her the disappointing news that he hadn't picked up. "Do you want to leave a message?"

"Yes. Ask him to call me on my cell phone the second he's able." She left her number before going into the bar for a soda. If she didn't hear from him within twenty minutes, then she'd have to go back to the town house.

Not five minutes passed before her phone rang. It sent her into a panic. For Nicky's sake, whatever she said to Pietra's brother, she had to be careful. Diplomatic.

She clicked on. "H-hello?"

"Julie Marchant?"

The way he said her name sounded foreign, and for

want of a better word, intimate. It sent a shockwave through her body.

"Yes. Thank you for calling me back."

"I didn't realize you'd phoned until I'd finished my shower." After a silence, he said, "We share a loss no one else could possibly understand, do we not?"

The tangible sorrow in his deep voice echoed her own agony. It opened the floodgates. "Yes." A sob escaped her throat. "I'm sorry," she whispered.

"Don't be. Since hearing the news, I've hardly been in control myself. Where are you exactly?"

Exactly? She swallowed hard. "In the bar of your hotel."

"Come up to my suite where we can talk in private." He gave her the number.

"Thank you. I'll be there in a minute."

She wiped the moisture off her face with a napkin. One last sip of cola for sustenance and she left the bar. The elevator let her off on his floor. Halfway down the hall she saw a man in a white polo shirt and tan khakis turn in her direction.

The clothes could have belonged to a thousand men, but the unconscious elegance of his stance, the way the material molded his broad shoulders and tall, lean body caused her mouth to go dry.

Even from the distance separating them, she could see he'd come from a scorching environment. His jet-black hair, combined with olive skin bronzed by the sun, took her breath.

Brows of the same black intensity framed his aquiline features. The proud nose and aggressive jaw sat well on such an unquestionably masculine face.

Her fascinated gaze fell helplessly to the lines of his wide, sensual mouth. Nicky's mouth! The baby's big size was no longer a mystery. He'd inherited his uncle's build, too. Every boy should be so lucky.

"What conclusions have you drawn?" came the silky question.

CHAPTER TWO

HEAT stole into Julie's cheeks to be caught staring like that. Of medium height, she had to tilt her head a ways. Their gazes collided. Midnight-black eyes stared back at her. Between their sadness and the shadows beneath them, she could see his pain.

"Forgive me. I was so busy picking out the similarities between you and Nicky, I didn't realize I was being rude."

"I confess to doing the same thing. Pietra sent me pictures of the baby. You two share the same golden hair. It's much lighter than your brother's."

"Nicky's will probably grow darker in time."

"Yours is like the sunlight finding a hole in the darkest canopy of the jungle floor."

She took an extra breath. "Is that a good thing?"

"*Sì, signorina.* A very good thing when you're slowly being devoured by a world of crawling green."

The image made her shiver.

"Come in."

"Thank you." As she walked past him, her elbow brushed against his arm, sending a different kind of sensation through her body. Her emotions, like her grief, were out of control.

They entered a lounge with some love seats and a table. She was too anxious to sit.

"Mr. Di Rocche—"

"Surely you can call me Massimo. Nicky's existence makes us relatives of a sort."

"Massimo, then—" she said a little breathlessly, smoothing her shoulder-length hair behind her ear. "I imagine you're wondering why I came here instead of waiting to meet you this evening."

A speculative look crossed his striking features, made even more prominent by suffering and fatigue. "Since you couldn't have known where I was unless your father told you, I'm assuming he revealed the contents of the will. If you're here on behalf of your family, begging me not to take Nicky away, I'm afraid it's out of my hands."

"I realize that."

Shawn and Pietra had made their wishes known through legal means. It appeared Massimo intended to honor them to the letter. Already she could see he wasn't the kind of man to tolerate interference when it came to his life, be it professional or personal.

He rubbed the back of his neck. "When I agreed to their wishes, I could never have contemplated this tragedy happening."

"No one could." Her voice shook.

"Tonight I'll make it clear to your family that I plan to bring Nicky back to the States for periodic visits. And naturally you're all welcome to visit him whenever you can."

She wanted to ask him where would that be *exactly*. She'd love to inquire if he expected her family to cut through a sea of vines with a machete in order to reach him and Nicky. But she didn't dare provoke him.

"That means a lot." Unfortunately her mother's worst fear would come to fruition when she heard the provisions of the will. Shawn and Pietra had really pulled the rug from under them. "However, I'm here for an entirely different reason."

He frowned. She felt his piercing gaze scrutinize her. It took all her willpower not to look away.

"I'll come straight to the point. Unless you got secretly married like Pietra, and she didn't choose to tell me you have a wife, then you're going to need help with Nicky for a while."

"*Naturalmente*. I've already made the arrangements."

"So fast?" she fired angrily.

His gaze turned wintry. "I'm in a hurry, Ms. Marchant."

"I'll just bet you are," she said through grated teeth. "It must have been quite an inconvenience to leave your precious dig and fly here to deal with a nephew you didn't even bother to see after Pietra had the baby."

Her comment produced a slight chiseling of his jaw. She realized she'd gone too far, but she couldn't help it. Her pain was acute.

"I think you'd better explain yourself," his voice rasped.

"I don't owe you anything."

Julie was so incensed, she had to get out of there before she said something unconscionable.

Though she was closer to the door, he reached it ahead of her with effortless male agility, blocking her exit.

"You came over here for a reason. I'd like to know what it is." His deceptively civil tone didn't fool her. Beneath those words lurked a demand.

The man was furious, and wouldn't allow her to leave without hearing an explanation first. If all the Di Rocches were as arrogant as her brother, it was no wonder Pietra had left Italy.

Heat stormed into her cheeks. "Would it do any good?" she challenged him.

"Try me," he mocked with unbearable hauteur.

"I was going to ask if you would hire me to be Nicky's nanny through this initial period of adjustment, however long it takes. That way I won't feel like I've lost him completely."

His dark brows elevated. She could hear his mind working. "I understand you have an excellent job in San Francisco."

"I do. But even before I heard the terms of the will, I'd planned to give it up to take care of Nicky."

He cocked his head. "If I'm not mistaken, you're involved with someone who works at the same company."

She shouldn't have been surprised Pietra had confided all that to her brother. They'd clearly been in closer touch than she'd thought.

"I was. It didn't work out," she muttered. "At this point nothing means more to me than Nicky. He needs constant love and security right now. He's missing his parents terribly."

His grim expression intensified. "Of course."

"When it comes to taking care of Nicky, not just any woman will do," she pointed out heatedly.

"This one has been a mother."

"Then that means she's an older woman. How will she fare in the jungle?" Julie cried. "I'm young and willing to live wherever you live. Nicky and I would adapt. Because of my job, which requires some travel, I have a passport. I'll get the necessary vaccinations."

His eyes played over her features. "What kind of work have you done?"

"It's a software company. On occasion I give presentations of the product to their foreign distributors. But to get back to Nicky, it's important for you to know that since he was born, I've tended him once a month on the weekends. We've started getting acquainted."

She was talking too fast, but she couldn't help it. The thought of him taking Nicky away was tearing her apart.

"As soon as I arrived here yesterday morning, I sent the babysitter home and have taken care of him myself. The poor little thing's sick."

He frowned. "How sick?"

"He's used to Pietra's milk. Last night he fought me on the bottle because he doesn't like formula. It upset him so much that he's developed a bad rash. This morning I had to call the doctor about it and get a prescription for him. Another day or two and it ought to clear up.

"But that isn't all that's wrong. He keeps looking for his parents. Introducing him to another stranger this soon will only frustrate him further. No other woman will ever love him the way I do. I'm beginning to gain his trust. Soon he'll learn to accept me."

Her eyes glazed with tears. "Even if Shawn and Pietra didn't consider me a proper guardian when they made out their will, I'd do anything for them. I loved them, and I adore Nicky. He's my brother's son. How could I not?"

With everything said, the last breath of air left her lungs. She waited, expecting him to say something. Anything! When he didn't, she felt like she was going to explode.

"*That's* what I came to say! But pleading my case to you is a lost cause isn't it? Mother was afraid Pietra's uncle would come for him and try to take him away from us. I thought she was being hysterical, but it turns out she was right! You're as awful as the rest of the Di Rocche clan."

His body stiffened, but she was too far gone to care.

"You're all in this together. The Italian big-boy network using all your money and position to close ranks on Shawn's son and turn him into a Di Rocche."

"Have you finished?" came the voice of ice.

Her hands formed fists. "No, I haven't even started. All this time you were in Central America you never had any use for Pietra, and you don't care a fig about Nicky. No doubt you'll have him dropped off at your uncle's where some built-in maid will change his diapers and give him bottles.

"In the walls of that prison he'll be taught to conform like the rest of the Di Rocche men, leaving you free to feed your addiction in Guatemala.

"You know what? You're the worst of them because Pietra trusted you—" Her voice rang out, but she didn't care.

"Your sister thought the world of you, even after you deserted her and left for Central America. She told me you only came to see her once before the baby was born. That's how much interest you had in their lives. And now you show up to do your uncle's dirty work. I think it's abominable."

"Are you quite through?" His eyes glittered dangerously.

"What's the matter? Can't you take the truth?" she said, baiting him. "If I've shocked you, I meant to, and I'll never apologize for the way I feel about Nicky."

She started for the door, then paused. "In case you're wondering, my parents have no idea I drove over here to see you. I don't intend for them to know I came. They're so devastated right now, if they knew how hard-hearted you really are it would destroy them."

Massimo let Shawn's grief-stricken sister charge out the door without trying to stop her. She'd obviously been in Pietra's confidence and knew enough to push one too many of Massimo's buttons.

This was a development he would never have envisioned. She was much more fragile than anyone knew. Not only wasn't she planning a wedding to her boyfriend, *she* was the one devastated by the terms of the will.

He needed to weigh everything carefully before he acted. A certain conversation with Pietra ran through his mind in vivid detail.

We've talked it over, brother dear. If, God forbid, anything should happen to us before Niccolo reaches eighteen, we would like you to be in charge of him. Will you agree?

Margaret's a good person. She means well, but Shawn's worried she'd be too possessive of him.

To ask Shawn's father would destroy his mother, never mind that he and his wife have their hands full with her autistic grandson.

That leaves Julie, the perfect choice, but she's on the brink of getting engaged. One day soon she'll be married and have children of her own. Shawn doesn't want her burdened. More importantly, he fears that Margaret would interfere with Julie's household and cause trouble. It could ruin her marriage.

I'm afraid you're the only one we can turn to in full confidence. You're the only person who could control Nicky's grandmother and still be fair to Shawn's family.

Since you're the only person Uncle Aldo can't control, we have no fear of his influence over our son.

In the meantime, it's a comfort to know you'll embrace our sweet Niccolo. With you guiding him, he'll lead a wonderful life. I realize it's asking a lot, but if anyone understands what it's like to live with someone besides your parents, you and I do.

Just remember this is only a precautionary measure. Nicky hasn't been born yet, and nothing's going to happen to Shawn and me. We've found love. We're going to live a long, happy life and have a big family.

But just in case…

On a groan, he reached for his cell phone. He'd promised to call his uncle. There was no question Pietra's death had affected the older man. He had to be suffering some remorse that there'd been no reconciliation. But such an event wouldn't have happened unless his uncle had made the first move.

Pietra had been too hurt by the dynamics inside their uncle's household. Now it was too late.

The doctor had advised him not to come to the funeral. It would put too much stress on his heart if he was hoping to recover. Massimo inhaled deeply.

How did anyone recover from this nightmare? He hadn't even seen the baby yet.

But Julie had,

No woman will ever love him the way I do.

He needs constant love and security.

He's missing his parents terribly.

Introducing him to another stranger this soon will only frustrate him further.

Despite her impassioned accusations, which had come home to roost, the torment in those smoky-blue eyes had reached down into Massimo's soul where anger over so many things lived.

"Uncle?"

"*Figlio mio.*" Aldo's voice trembled. "Have you seen her?"

He closed his eyes tightly, but nothing would shut out the image. "Yes. I've just come from the mortuary."

His uncle cleared his throat several times. "I'd hoped to be there and see her boy."

Massimo remained unconvinced on that score. "You'll get your chance."

"Dr. Zampoli says it won't be for a while."

"The good doctor doesn't know everything."

"What do you mean?"

A shudder wracked his body. "I'm coming back to Italy, Uncle."

"For how long?"

"Long enough."

"Don't feed me lies, Massimo." The excitement in his voice was tangible. "I can take them from anyone but you."

"If you don't believe me, ask Guido. He and Lia are getting the villa ready in Bellagio."

"What's wrong with my house?"

His lips compressed. It hadn't taken two seconds for his uncle to start dictating. "I want Nicky to be raised in his grandparents' home."

A long silence ensued before his uncle blurted, "*You* have custody of the boy?"

His uncle's shock brought a satisfied curl to Massimo's mouth. "That's right."

The older man wanted Massimo home running the business, but not under these circumstances. A baby in residence frustrated the plans he'd orchestrated for Massimo's destiny years earlier.

"I know the perfect woman to look after him."

Of course he did, and Massimo knew exactly who it was. Everyone knew. His uncle was as transparent as the cat who'd licked all the cream. But such a split-second recovery explained the envy on the part of his business rivals.

"So do I, Uncle." Pietra had called her sister-in-law the perfect choice. Massimo had just been presented with living proof that Julie Marchant loved the baby to the point she was willing to fight to the death for him.

No other person besides himself would place Nicky's welfare above every other consideration. Such a demonstration proved beyond doubt he could trust her with their nephew.

A few e-mail photos didn't do justice to her slenderly rounded figure. Like her brother she possessed those classic features reminiscent of the Swedish blood in their ancestry. They were exceptionally good-looking people.

The existence of Shawn's golden-blond sister on the premises would add a new component to an old equation, ensuring a different outcome he wouldn't allow his uncle to manipulate.

"You don't know how long I've been waiting for this day, Massimo."

But for a horrendous tragedy, his uncle would have been forced to wait forever.

"I'll let you know when I've arrived in Milan."

"When's the funeral?"

"Graveside services are planned for the day after tomorrow."

"Good. That gives Dante and Lazio time to get there."

For Pietra's sake Massimo was glad to hear his cousins were coming to represent the family, even if it was only upon his uncle's orders. Massimo was even happier that Sansone wouldn't be with them. When he wasn't there to order his younger brothers around, there wasn't as much tension.

"I'll reserve rooms for them."

"Excellent. I told them to take the company jet. Now that I know you're coming home with the baby, you're going to need it."

For once Massimo agreed with his uncle. The thought of taking a five-month-old baby halfway around the world on a commercial airliner had been a daunting one.

"Mind the doctor, Uncle. *Ciao.*"

The selfish part of Massimo would like nothing better than to continue working at his favorite hobby with his nephew in tow, but he'd made a promise to Shawn and Pietra. The jungle was no place to take a baby. Maybe in Nicky's teens.

Julie hadn't been far off. His hobby *was* an addiction.

But for now his nephew deserved everything Massimo could give him. As she had said, he needed love most of all. Being his aunt, she would always provide that, even after Massimo didn't need her help anymore.

Until that day came—a day he couldn't think about right now—they would figure things out as they went. Though he was considerably older, she knew a hell of a lot more about babies than he did. He'd never even changed a diaper.

Unfortunately for Nicky, he was stuck with a substitute father he hadn't even met yet. Massimo assumed the rest would fall into place in time. How difficult could it be to give a baby a bottle?

Speaking of which, he took some water from the bar's minifridge to quench his thirst. Old habits died hard.

Fifteen minutes later he arrived at the town house and knocked. Behind the front door he could hear an infant wailing.

Niccolo…

The sound tore at his gut, making his pain excruciatingly real.

Mr. Marchant opened the door. Beyond his shoulder Massimo could see Julie's mother. He recognized them from pictures. Both were dark blond. Attractive. She was walking around with the baby, trying to calm him down. There was no sign of Julie.

"We meet at last, Massimo. Come in."

* * *

"Kendra? This is Julie again."

"Oh, hi!"

Relieved the cute teenager was home she said, "Do you know any tricks to help us? Nicky just keeps crying. Even my mother can't get him to stop. Before I call the doctor again, I thought I'd find out what you do to help him settle down."

"Try the little musical swing they bought last month. He likes that."

"Where is it?"

"It should be right by the rocker."

"I don't see it, but I'll look around. Thanks for the tip."

"Sure. The poor little thing. Good luck."

Julie knew for a fact she hadn't seen it anywhere in the house. Maybe the back patio?

She hurried down the stairs. Her heart skipped a beat to discover Massimo in the front room with her parents. The tension was thick. When had he come? After what had transpired at the hotel, she'd been dreading this moment.

Her father made the introductions while Massimo held an out-of-control Nicky in his strong arms. For a brief moment their eyes met. She expected to read fury in his. Instead his whole expression was enigmatic, throwing her off balance.

To complicate her feelings even more, his Italian features mesmerized her. She got a fluttering sensation in her chest before rushing out the back door of the kitchen.

Sure enough the swing was sitting next to the wrought-iron table and chairs. She brought it inside and carried it into the living room. "Let's try this."

While Massimo set the baby inside it and fiddled with the straps, she knelt down to turn on the various switches. "Kendra says you like this. Let's find out, shall we?"

The music began to play, but Nicky's crying only grew

louder. There was no motion. "It's not moving. Maybe it's broken."

"I'll do it by hand," Massimo murmured, getting down on his haunches, accidentally bringing their arms and thighs together. Julie pretended not to notice the contact even though she felt it through every cell of her body.

Though his chin wobbled and there were a lot of hiccups, by some miracle Nicky eventually quieted down.

Bless Kendra.

"I believe you've got it going," her father said.

Massimo let go of the seat to test it. Sure enough, the swing was doing its job.

Julie let out a heavy sigh and stood up.

She happened to glance at Massimo, who'd risen to his full, intimidating height. "Mission accomplished," he whispered. Along with the sorrow she caught a glint of relief in his eyes. Again she felt stirrings inside her that made no sense, not when he was the enemy.

"I can't imagine what Shawn and Pietra were thinking when they gave you custody of our grandson. Central America is no place for him. Furthermore you know nothing about raising a child."

Good for her mom! With that opus she'd gone for the jugular. Though her hostility wasn't going to help anything, as Julie had already found out, she *was* saying all the things Julie felt.

"I happen to agree with you on both points," he responded quietly. "That's why I'm taking him back to Italy."

"While you traipse off to the jungle once more, leaving him to strangers who won't care one whit for him?"

"Margaret—"

"It's all right," Massimo said, eyeing Julie's parents. "If

my life had been different, archaeology would have been my career, not a hobby. As it stands, I'll be returning to take my place in the family business."

What? Julie reeled.

Pietra had indicated her brother would never go back. Julie didn't believe him for a minute!

"Nicky will be living with me in the home where Pietra and I were born," he continued. "Before their deaths our parents lived in Bellagio on Lake Como, only a short distance from the office in Milan.

"The villa is Nicky's heritage. My staff will be devoted to him. They're getting things prepared for him as we speak."

"But the people who love him are here," her mother asserted, not the least swayed by the trappings. "He'll be surrounded by strange faces."

She'd taken the words out of Julie's mouth. She could only applaud her mom.

"I was hoping to solve that problem by hiring your daughter for a while." His glance switched to Julie with a complacent gleam that caused the hairs to stand on the back of her neck.

"That is if you're willing, *and* if you're able to leave your work, of course. Pietra told me you've spent time with Nicky, which means you're not a complete stranger to him like I am."

The world stilled while she almost fainted from shock. Her parents looked equally nonplussed.

His gaze continued to bore into hers. She felt its disturbing penetration to the marrow of her bones. "How would you feel about helping me with our nephew until he's used to his new home? Your mother's right. I know nothing about babies."

He knew exactly how Julie felt about it!

Not by one flicker of those dark lashes did he give away the fact that she'd paid a visit to his hotel room earlier. His discretion was only eclipsed by his cunning.

A shiver ran up her spine. To turn him down now would prove to him she hadn't meant what she'd said. Yet to tell him she'd like the nanny job meant putting herself in a position where he'd exact retribution at some later time for her meltdown in his hotel room. Julie hadn't known real fear until this moment.

"I love Nicky," she said quietly. "There's nothing I wouldn't do for him. Resigning from my job will be no problem." He already knew that. For some inexplicable reason he'd decided to grant her the wish of her heart. "Before we knew about the will, I'd planned to take care of my nephew."

"I think it's a terrific idea," came her father's heartfelt comment. "Don't you, Margaret?"

"I…I suppose it is. I'm just having a hard time comprehending it."

A faint smile of satisfaction broke the corner of Massimo's hard, sensuous mouth. Julie had made a surreptitious study of it. The description seemed a contradiction in terms, yet both applied.

To her parents it might look like he was truly relieved someone else close to Nicky would share the burden with him. Julie knew differently.

"Pietra told me you have an important position with a software company in San Francisco—" he kept speaking to her. "Perhaps they'll give you a leave of absence. If not, you won't need to worry. I'll be paying you considerably more for your time."

She swallowed hard, unable to credit what she was hearing.

His eyes swerved to her parents who were still visibly stunned. "Naturally my home will be yours whenever you wish to visit Nicky. Come often and stay as long as you want. On holidays I'll bring him to California and Hawaii. Nicky needs his grandparents. For his sake, we'll make it work."

The magic words.

Julie's mother teared up. Her father patted him on the shoulder. "Indeed we will."

Once more Massimo turned to Julie. "Pietra mentioned a boyfriend. He's welcome at the villa, too. Anytime he wants to fly over to see you."

She'd told him that relationship had ended, but he'd thrown that in for effect to make everything sound convincing. Nothing escaped his steel-trap mind. Within minutes he'd accomplished what Julie hadn't thought possible—

He'd silenced her mother and reassured her parents they hadn't lost Nicky. In the process he'd caught Julie before her life hit rock bottom, but she knew in her bones he meant to extract a price for the accusations she'd hurtled at him.

She looked down at the baby, who was finally asleep again. Knowing she'd be traveling to Italy with him took away some of the sting of the will's contents. Enough to help her get through the graveside services they had facing them.

But in its place an indefinable fear had taken hold and wouldn't let go.

CHAPTER THREE

THE spacious well-lit Di Rocche jet with its panoramic windows could hold fourteen passengers plus the crew. Once they'd taken off, and the lights from San Francisco receded into the night, Julie was scarcely aware of Massimo's rather austere, well-dressed cousins, who did business in the aft conference compartment.

Though deferential to Massimo and very correct with her family throughout the service and afterward, for the most part they kept to themselves.

From the little Massimo had told her, Dante was thirty-nine and Lazio forty-two. Both were married and had children. His forty-four-year-old cousin, Sansone, hadn't come. He, too, had children, one of them in college. All of them held responsible positions within the company.

So many stern males who had no time for Pietra must have been daunting to her. She'd only been eight to Massimo's thirteen when they'd lost their parents.

Massimo talked off and on with his brown-haired cousins, but for the most part he stayed in the berthable cabin with her and Nicky. An alarming prospect because she never knew at what moment he was going to pull off the gloves. Her anxiety while she waited made her feverish.

Hopefully, with Nicky right next to them, she didn't have to worry about it during the flight. Up to now the baby had been pretty good all things considered. But after refueling in New York for the last leg of the flight to Milan, he'd started to fuss.

Julie didn't think he could be hungry again. With a steward aboard to bring their meals and heat his bottles, she'd never known such luxury.

Everything had been provided for her and the baby's comfort.

Luckily his rash had improved. A few more days using the special cream and the last of the redness would be gone.

This was the first time she and Massimo had been on their own with Nicky. Until they'd boarded the jet, Julie's mother and father had taken turns tending the baby. She knew their hearts were broken at the thought of him leaving the country.

Though Massimo possessed a commanding air of authority that would be intimidating to most people, he hadn't tried to interfere or take over with her parents, for which Julie had been grateful. Pain clung to all of them like a dark mist. The airport scene represented the end of the Marchant family the way they'd always known it. Nothing would ever be the same again.

Not for Massimo, either, she had to concede.

Whatever the true nature of their relationship, a drunk driver had killed Pietra, the person closest to him. He'd been uprooted from his work to return to a place where he didn't want to go, to take on a baby he didn't know.

Even if he was Nicky's uncle and already felt a bond with him, by virtue of them being family, to take on guardianship of him overnight had to be a daunting prospect. Yet he'd done it without hesitation.

Pietra had idolized her brother. Though Julie was suspicious of his motives when it came to her, she could understand the reason for his sister's adoration.

While other people stood around in a crisis wringing their hands, Massimo saw what needed doing and did it with the ease of urbane sophistication any male would kill to possess. Julie's father had welcomed Massimo's help with all the decisions.

She tried to imagine Brent in similar circumstances and couldn't. No matter his age, Massimo would have handled everything with unmatchable mastery.

Because he was a *man*.

While Shawn had been in Italy on business for the winery, he'd told Julie he'd seen the Di Rocche logo everywhere. It meant rock, a symbol for something solid, unshakeable. The Di Rocche family could have coined it after Massimo. He was the rock you could instinctively count on.

Pietra had counted on him. So had Shawn, who must have been convinced of his brother-in-law's underlying integrity, otherwise he wouldn't have considered giving him legal custody of Nicky should the unthinkable happen.

To everyone's horror it *had* happened. Lives had been forever changed, especially Nicky's. He would never know his parents. Life could be so unfair. Julie swallowed another sob.

Maybe the baby sensed her overwhelming sadness and that's why he started to cry in earnest. Throughout her contemplation of the incredibly attractive man seated across from her, he'd worked himself up.

"What do you suppose is wrong?" Massimo asked, ever attentive despite the fatigue lines etching his hard-boned features. The steward had just cleared away their breakfast trays.

She was tempted to reply that the baby wanted Shawn and Pietra, but of course he knew that. Instead she said, "He might need to burp, but I imagine he's missing his own bed."

"Aren't we all."

"It would take a big hammock for a man your size," she said without thinking.

IIis lips twisted. "You've watched too many Indiana Jones films. These days we use cots." He got to his feet and reached for Nicky. "You need a break. I'll take him for a walk. Hopefully it will distract him."

The baby looked so tiny in his uncle's arms. Julie glanced away in an effort to block out the sight of his well-defined chest covered in a pearl-gray cotton sweater.

The open neck revealed a tanned column of throat. She could tell there was a fine dusting of hair, as well. His sleeves were pulled up to the elbows, revealing the hard sinews of his forearms.

Expelling a controlled breath, she decided now would be a good time to use the restroom. Her hair needed a good brushing. She could refresh her lipstick.

When she returned to her seat a few minutes later, she was surprised to discover he'd come back. Nicky lay facedown across his powerful thighs encased in expensive-looking charcoal trousers. Using a bronzed hand to rub the baby's back, Massimo had managed to quiet him.

"I should have thought of that. I'm jealous."

One corner of his so very male mouth curved, causing her pulse to race. Since she'd first met him outside his hotel room, it had been doing that on a regular basis despite her reservations about him.

"We can thank Dante. He told me to try it."

"How old are his children?"

"Fourteen and seventeen. I presume having been a father twice, it's like riding a bicycle. Once you've learned, you never forget."

"Did all your cousins marry young?"

His black eyes flickered over her. "My uncle insisted on it. Their wives were handpicked."

"Judging from your bachelor status, you were the only one not afraid of him."

"He wasn't *my* father. Though the strictures of Uncle Aldo's household could be daunting, to a certain degree I was able to get away with being a nonconformist. Much to my cousins' chagrin," he added on a more sober note.

"Like what, for instance?" Her curiosity was going to get the better of her.

"He believes an unmarried man past twenty-one is a menace to society."

"Uh-oh. Did your aunt have any say in the matter?"

"None. It didn't help that she was sickly throughout their marriage and needed waiting on. She died a year after Pietra and I went to live with them."

How completely different from Julie's family, where her mother's need to be in charge had eventually beaten down her father.

"I thought it was the other way around in Italian households."

He studied her through shuttered eyes. "You watch too many made-for-TV movies."

"According to you I watch too many movies period."

His brief white smile caused her insides to dissolve. "I'll concede the point."

"Was Pietra a rebel, too?"

"Afraid so. She took after me," he admitted ruefully. "No

one was going to do her choosing for her. I wasn't surprised when she told me she'd fallen in love with Shawn."

Julie's throat swelled. "Pietra was the best thing that ever happened to my brother. They didn't have very long together, but they were two of the happiest people I've ever seen. She wasn't intimidated by our mother."

"Our uncle did a good job of preparing her in that department." His remarks kept hinting at a dark history.

"Does he live in Bellagio, too?"

"No."

That was definitive enough. The one-syllable answer filled her with relief.

"Wh-what about your cousins?"

The furrow between his black brows deepened. "No need to worry. The Di Rocche family are Milan born and bred. My mother came from Bellagio."

"Pietra showed me pictures of your parents when they were very young. Your mother was a great beauty. Were those their wedding photos?"

The second she asked the question, his hand stilled on Nicky's back for a moment before he said no.

Without more of an explanation, it was clear the discussion was over. The sudden tension radiating from him made her mouth go dry. If Massimo had no wish to volunteer anything else, that was his prerogative.

Feeling uneasy, she got to her feet. "The baby's fallen asleep." She quickly lifted him off Massimo's legs and fastened him back in the seat harness of his baby carrier.

After covering him with a light blanket, she sat down again. "If I've irritated you by asking questions, I…I apologize. Having come from a divorced home, I prefer to keep certain family matters private myself."

No one understood that better than Julie, who loathed having to discuss her parents' breakup with anyone. She certainly couldn't blame him about his reticence in that regard.

Yet the second the words left her lips, she realized how ludicrous she must sound after the aspersions she'd cast on him the first time they'd met and had yet to apologize for.

He studied her through brooding eyes. "As you so succinctly reminded me at the hotel, I come from a Machiavellian world, one I'd hoped to have put behind me. You enter it at your own risk."

Her heart missed a beat. "Are you saying you had another agenda for hiring me? Like for instance using me to test your tea before you drink it?" She wanted an honest answer from him, but had couched it to sound tongue-in-cheek.

Some of the frown lines relaxed. "I didn't mean to imply anything quite that sinister. But I will ask your compliance in one regard. I expect you to come to me if something doesn't seem right, or if someone makes you uncomfortable."

He was serious! Her heart picked up speed.

"By someone you mean—"

"Anyone in the family," he supplied. "While you're in Italy you'll be living under my roof where my rules apply. No one else's. Understood?" The question veiled an implicit demand.

"Yes. Of course."

"You can trust Guido and Lia. They run the villa."

Julie was starting to get confused. Everything he said and did was putting cracks in her mind-set.

"If the climate is that fraught with intrigue, why are you taking Nicky back there?" So much for not asking more questions.

He gave an elegant shrug of his shoulders. "This is his Italian birthright, the one I can help him claim. When he's old enough, I'll make certain he explores his American roots. By giving me guardianship, his parents made it clear they wanted him comfortable in both worlds."

Shawn and Pietra couldn't ask for more than that, where their son was concerned.

The longer she was around Massimo, the less she realized she understood or knew. Much as she hated to admit it, she found him the most fascinating—and infuriating—man she'd ever met. There had to be many women who felt the same way.

But she was way off base to be entertaining thoughts about Pietra's brother of all people. He was an educated, wealthy, experienced man of the world, ten years older than she. To think for one second he'd be interested in her was beyond imagining.

Shocked by her wandering thoughts while another part of her was waiting for the real Massimo to exact his revenge, she stared down at Nicky. "He's been surprisingly good so far."

"I'd say we haven't done too badly."

His comment brought a sad smile to her lips because it suddenly dawned on her that no matter his ulterior reason for allowing her to come with him and Nicky, Massimo had more faith in her than her own brother.

She darted him a quick glance. "That's true, but we haven't even landed yet."

"We've started our descent to Linate Airport. The light just flashed on."

So it had. They would be touching down in Milan before she knew it. Julie could scarcely comprehend she and Nicky were about to enter the world of the Di Rocches.

After making certain he was secure in his harness, she fastened her own seat belt. Through veiled lashes she watched Massimo strap himself in. The play of muscle in his arms and chest drew her gaze. He had an incredible physique. Julie trembled to realize *he* was incredible.

While she castigated herself for her growing weakness, the jet glided to a stop on the tarmac. The next few minutes became a blur as Massimo gathered up Nicky's things. His cousins preceded them out the door of the jet. She followed, carrying a sleepy Nicky in her arms.

In the next instant, two things happened. While a chauffeur from one of the waiting limos relieved Massimo of the baby's paraphernalia, a voluptuous woman with long legs stepped out of the other crying Massimo's name.

Her red hair flowed halfway down the back of her designer suit. She swept past his cousins to throw her arms around his neck. The press of their mouths and bodies bespoke a prior intimacy.

It all happened so fast it was too late for Julie to shut her eyes. She feared the sight of their embrace would always remain emblazoned on her consciousness.

Dante glanced at Julie, who'd managed to reach the bottom step without stumbling. With her hair caught back in a ponytail, she could imagine the unfavorable impression she made in comparison, wearing jeans and a cotton top Nicky had snuggled against most of the flight.

Mortified to think Dante might be able to tell that her heart felt like it had been sliced with a newly sharpened knife, she flashed him a breezy smile. "Thanks for your earlier suggestion. When Massimo laid the baby across his legs, Nicky settled right down."

He gave a slight bow of acknowledgment. "While my cousin's otherwise occupied with Seraphina, let me assist you."

The implication being that Massimo might be a while. She'd already assumed as much.

After opening the door, he fastened Nicky's baby carrier inside on the base. Julie sank down next to the baby. Though she could claim exhaustion after such a long journey, it was something else entirely different that had brought on this weakness.

"Thank you," she murmured, trying desperately to forget what was going on behind the limo.

He shrugged. "Pietra was family. Have fun on your vacation."

The door closed.

Vacation? Was that what Massimo had told his cousins? That she was only going to be here for a short visit?

Up to now the Di Rocche family had said and done all the proper things, yet their cold natures had made her feel expendable. Especially just now. To say "have fun" to her while she was still grieving sounded deliberate and cruel on his part. His gross lack of sensitivity hurt.

If he and Lazio had always been like this, she could understand why Pietra had clung to Massimo growing up. His departure for Central America explained the reason she'd gravitated to Shawn's warmth.

While Julie sat there waiting for Massimo to get in the car, she had to accept the fact that Pietra hadn't been the only woman adversely affected by his decision to work in another part of the world.

And that thought led to other depressing thoughts about the women he'd left behind in Guatemala. There would definitely have been someone, maybe several beautiful, exotic types.

Despite his bachelor status, a thirty-four-year-old man like Massimo hadn't lived a celibate life. Nor would he care about Julie's past relationships. So how absurd was it of her to have feelings, let alone be jealous of his? Except in her capacity to help care for Nicky, she meant nothing to him.

If she wanted to keep her position, she'd better act the part of a nanny whose only job was to look after the baby. After her initial castigations about him and his family, he clearly wouldn't tolerate her asking personal questions or making more judgments. In truth, she wasn't entitled.

With a new sense of determination to keep herself focused on her only reason for being here, she took advantage of the quiet time to change Nicky.

"You're such a sweetheart," she said after laying him on the little pad folded in the baby bag. "Let's see if that cream is still doing its job."

Massimo chose that moment to climb in the opposite door. He'd brought the scent of Seraphina's perfume with him. "Sorry to keep you waiting."

Except for an apology, he made no explanation. She'd expected none.

"We're not in a hurry," she said without looking at him. After applying the cream, she finished diapering Nicky.

Massimo leaned forward. "His rash seems better."

"I think so, too. Aren't we glad." She kissed Nicky's tummy. He rewarded her with the sweetest smile.

Having become quite expert at changing him by now, she was able to snap up his little stretchy suit with no problem. The pretense of competency was something to cling to.

"One more short flight in the helicopter and we'll be home."

Massimo's neutral tone told her nothing about his true feelings lurking beneath the surface. Remembering the woman whose arms he'd just left, they couldn't be all bad.

"Did you hear that, Nicky? We're going for another ride." In the family helicopter no less. She placed him back in the infant seat. The limo began to move, and by the time she'd put everything else away, they'd reached the helipad.

Massimo took charge of Nicky. Soon she and the baby were ensconced behind him and the pilot. Once their things were stowed on board and introductions made, they took off. The sudden lift caused her stomach to lurch. After a few minutes, however, she grew used to the motion.

Her first helicopter ride over Milan would have been enough to rave about, but the sights filling her vision as they neared Lake Como defied description. What might appear commonplace to them was like being transported to another planet for Julie.

She fastened hungry eyes on the shoreline dotted with tiny ochre towns so picture perfect, she had to be dreaming. From the deepest blue water she'd ever seen rose forested slopes that ended in mountain peaks covered in snow.

At Massimo's instruction the pilot swept lower so she could pick out olive and palm trees, bougainvillea, even rhododendrons and azaleas growing in a profusion of riotous color. They'd flown into a subtropical paradise.

Soon a picturesque town appeared, whose colorful houses and narrow streets were almost completely surrounded by water. Among the lush greenery she spied palatial villas with terraced gardens and cypress trees covering the foot of the terrain.

As a gasp of sheer delight escaped her lips, she felt a pair of black eyes trained on her. "Bellagio's renowned for being the most beautiful town in Europe."

She turned her head toward Massimo, who was looking over his shoulder at her. "I…I can't find the words to describe what I'm seeing. Pietra's love for Shawn must have been overpowering to turn her back on this kind of beauty."

"The Sonoma vineyards have their own brand of charm."

"That's true, but nothing I've ever seen or imagined compares to this." She quickly averted her eyes.

No man I've ever met compares to you.

The helicopter dipped lower until it hovered near a gold-tinged villa surrounded by a sun-drenched garden hugging the steep hillside.

Her breath caught. "Your home?"

He nodded solemnly. The helicopter set them down in a cleared space at the rear of the villa.

"Oh, Nicky—" she cried in absolute wonder. "To think this is where your mommy grew up, where *you're* going to live—"

As Massimo had pointed out, this was Nicky's birthright.

It was so fabulous only a fool would have asked him why he was bringing the baby back here. She cringed over her pathetic naiveté.

Yet for all her euphoria, she wasn't wrong to feel trepidation. She knew from Massimo's history that this particular Garden of Eden had its serpent. What frightened her more was anticipating the moment when it would strike without warning.

After thanking Guido for setting up a new crib and dresser, Massimo went in search of Lia. Per his instructions, they'd made one adjustment to the rooms on the second floor.

Pietra's bedroom would now serve as the nursery. Julie would stay in the adjoining suite. Massimo's was down the hall. The arrangement would give them both easy access to the baby without his having to go through Julie's room first.

Rounding the corner, he found Lia leaving Julie's suite with a tray. He noted with satisfaction that she'd eaten most of her lunch.

Over the past week she'd displayed little appetite. Ironically he'd been more worried about her than Nicky, who'd finally started drinking his formula without problem. After several failed attempts in the beginning with Julie looking on, Massimo learned that all he had to do was act in charge and plunge the nipple in Nicky's mouth. Suddenly the baby stopped fighting him and they were in business. At that point Massimo didn't know who was more surprised.

"Congratulations," she'd said. "You've stumbled onto the secret of the assertive doctrine, just like I did."

Between her gentle laughter and a smile for Nicky that drew his attention to the passionate curve of her mouth, he felt a sense of accomplishment he hadn't experienced in years.

He popped a lone grape from her plate into his mouth. "Did Julie mention needing anything else right now?"

"No. The *signorina* put the baby in his carryall next to her bed. Both are asleep. She cares for him like he's her own *bambino*." Lia's eyes misted over. "Such a beautiful child Pietra made. To think she's gone."

Massimo inhaled sharply, not wanting to dwell on the nightmare they'd just lived through. It still enveloped him like a shroud.

"I'm going to bed, myself. Have Gina bring him to me when he's awake, no matter the hour. Julie needs her sleep. I'll feed him."

She nodded.

"*Bene. Grazie*, Lia."

"*Momento*, Massimo. Cesar urged you to call him at your convenience. He and Luca sent flowers. I put them in your study."

"I need to get hold of them." Cesar and his elder brother, Luca, would be shocked when they learned Nicky would be living in Italy with Massimo. This would especially impact Cesar because it meant Massimo's bachelor existence had come to an end. The fallout from Pietra's fatal accident was still reverberating.

"You've had many other phone calls. Your uncle, Signor Vercelli, Signor Ricci, Seraphina Ricci, Dottor Pittman, Dottor Reese and Signor Walton."

He checked his stride. "Walton?"

"Signorina Marchant's fiancé. He sounded anxious to speak to her. Something to do with a wedding, but it was a poor connection."

Massimo frowned. So it wasn't over. Whatever quarrel they'd had, the poor devil had to be kicking himself by now.

"I'll tell her. The rest of them will have to wait."

Especially his uncle, who'd already played his first hand to no avail. Making sure Seraphina was at the airport to greet him the second he stepped off the plane hadn't come as any surprise.

His uncle and her father had been plotting an alliance between the two of them for the past four years. But Massimo wasn't in love with her. Even if he had been, he would never have married her. She was a big-city girl, overly indulged by her papa and his money. Unsuited to live in a third-world country.

Totally unlike Julie, for instance.

Disturbed by thoughts that kept turning to her, he headed down the hall. Upon reaching his bedroom, his legs, in fact his whole body, felt like lead. Since the phone call from Sansone which seemed a hundred years ago, he hadn't truly slept.

He showered but was too tired to shave. However, once he was in his old bed, his brain wouldn't shut off. Like bubbles that kept popping, one thought led to another. Damn if the woman sleeping down the hall hadn't gotten beneath his skin.

Massimo could still see her standing there trembling in his hotel room while she railed against his family. In one breath she attacked, in the next she begged to be a part of Nicky's life, insisting they would adapt to the jungle if they had to. He figured she would have said anything in her grief in order to be with the baby.

He still thought that, but having spent some time with her, he was also convinced she'd do whatever she had to and never complain about it. His mouth curved to imagine the stir those two blond heads would create among the natives as his loaded canoe glided deeper into the forest…

With her aboard the jet helping him with Nicky, their flight across two continents and an ocean had been surprisingly enjoyable. The insulation from his cousins had been another plus. He'd hardly given them a thought while he and Julie kept Nicky and each other occupied. She was intelligent. Unspoiled. It was almost as if the three of them were their own little family.

To his shock he found himself missing the intimacy of the plane's interior. In such close proximity, he hadn't needed an excuse to look at her whenever he wanted. He'd been attracted to her at the hotel, and was even more so now.

Long lashes darker than her hair fringed wide-set blue eyes. His gaze studied the perfect oval of her face, then drifted over a generous mouth to her well-shaped body.

The image of Nicky snuggled up against fresh youthful skin with her gold hair splayed across the headrest wouldn't leave his mind.

It was true what Lia had said moments ago. Julie was acting very much like a mother. His housekeeper had been prepared to look after Nicky herself, but how could she do anything when Julie put the baby in the same room with her?

He had a feeling that consciously or not, this sort of thing was going to keep happening. Time wouldn't change Julie's feelings for Nicky, only deepen them, ensuring an unbreakable bond.

If he hadn't brought Julie with him, Lia and the maids would be the ones seeing to most of Nicky's needs. There'd be no danger in them forming an attachment to him, or Nicky to them. On the contrary. His tiny nephew needed people around him he could grow to love and trust.

Yet if Massimo were honest with himself, he had to admit the help wouldn't curl up with Nicky and play with him the same way she did. Every child deserved that kind of love and attention.

Unfortunately, Julie would be leaving at some point—her relationship with Walton clearly wasn't as over as she'd made it out. He hadn't consciously thought about it, but now the prospect of that eventuality alarmed him. For the baby to lose her at any given time would be like losing a second mother.

It had only been ten days, yet already Massimo had grown used to her being there to help him with Nicky, who appeared to adore her. He groaned, haunted by the possibility he'd made a mistake in letting her come to Italy.

In retrospect he shouldn't have allowed his compassion for her pain to get to him. Those drenched blue eyes half despising him for being named guardian had caught him off guard in the hotel room. That, and her obvious love for the baby.

Normally he didn't make errors in judgment like this. Being unencumbered by marriage, he'd had the freedom to immerse himself in his archaeological pursuits. That was the way he'd planned it long ago. Even if he was back in Italy, he had every intention of working on the book he'd started in his spare time.

He punched his pillow, but no amount of rearranging made him more comfortable. There wasn't any way around the fact that Nicky wasn't the only one who'd developed a bond with Julie. Something had to be done before things went too far.

According to Julie's watch it was four in the afternoon Bellagio time. She and Nicky had been asleep for hours. Both their clocks were off, but it didn't matter. He was being the best boy on earth right now!

She'd taken a shower before getting in bed; however, he still needed a bath. "Let's try the sink, shall we?"

Julie set out a towel and clean diaper, then filled the marble basin halfway.

"Here we go." She lowered his wiggly body into the warm water. He immediately began kicking. "You love that, don't you?"

She couldn't help but wonder if any baby had ever had a bath in surroundings that looked as though a princess lived here. Except for loving parents, Pietra and Massimo had lacked for none of the monetary things of life. History had repeated itself with Nicky.

Julie fought back tears. "As soon as we've finished and I've given you a bottle, we'll go exploring." The sight of the town from the helicopter had been so glorious, she couldn't wait any longer. After they came back she'd unpack everything and get settled.

Ten minutes later he'd drunk most of his formula and they were both ready to go. She'd dressed in a pair of pleated tan pants and a short-sleeved white top. After arranging her hair in a loose knot, she put on a coat of frosted-pink lipstick, then dressed Nicky. He looked adorable in a little blue play suit with a superhero motif on the bib.

"Now for this new hip sling."

It was a padded pouch affair in khaki twill to cushion his legs while she walked around with him. After buying some things before leaving Sonoma, the clerk had convinced her to get one.

"They're the latest rage for tourists with a baby. Easy to pack and don't take up much room." Julie figured that until Massimo bought Nicky a stroller, it was perfect.

She left the room and made her way downstairs to the elegant foyer, where she saw one of the maids she'd met earlier.

"Gina? I'm going out for a walk. Please let Lia know."

"Have you told the *signore*?"

"No. I haven't seen him. Is there a problem?"

The last thing she wanted was for Massimo to think she was waiting for him at every turn. Julie had been the one to beg for this job. Though he'd hired her to be Nicky's nanny, she was never at ease with him.

For her own peace of mind, the less she saw of him the better. It would be disastrous if on top of her secret fear of him, he knew how attracted she was to him.

Gina looked concerned. "He left instructions I should bring Niccolo to him."

"I'll do it then. Where is he?"

"No…no…" She spread her hands. "The *signore* is sleeping."

Julie wasn't surprised. She was sure he hadn't gotten any sleep on the plane. "Then he shouldn't be disturbed. I'll be back in an hour. He won't even know we've been gone."

Gina didn't seem pleased about the idea, but Julie wasn't about to sit around until he got up. Waiting made you think. She'd already done too much thinking and looking at Massimo on the plane.

Now that she was in Italy, she planned to keep herself and Nicky so busy Massimo's anger with her would pass. Since that terrible moment in his hotel room, she didn't think she'd done anything else to arouse his wrath, but she couldn't be sure. Nicky had to be her first priority now.

CHAPTER FOUR

ONCE Julie slipped out the door of the villa, she stopped to breathe in the scent of flowers filling the balmy air.

Paradise found. She wondered if Milton had come here.

The villa faced out on the terraced stone stairway leading down to gardens filled with camellias and orange trees. Cypress trees delineating the property stood tall against the vista of Lake Como and the colorful town below.

Massimo had pointed out several famous eighteenth- and nineteenth-century villas to her before they'd landed in the grounds of his villa. It might be smaller, but as far as she was concerned his home stood out on the lower hillside like a jewel in a gem-studded crown.

Where to go first? The delights of the grounds called to her, but she could enjoy them anytime while she lived here. After the long flight, she was anxious to get her bearings along with some much needed exercise.

Opting for the side stairs off the deep porch, she made her way to the courtyard that led to the main road. Almost at the gate, she noticed an open top sports car turn in, the kind Brent would have killed to own. She quickly moved out of its way.

The light-brown-haired man at the wheel pulled over and got out wearing shorts and a tight-fitting body shirt. He was her brother's height and looked to be about her own age. His hooded brown eyes reminded her of Lazio's. They swept over her in male admiration.

"Good afternoon, *signorina*. You have to be Pietra's sister-in-law, Julie," he said in excellent English. "I had no idea you were so *bellissima*."

"I'm afraid you have me at a disadvantage." His flirtatious manner reminded her of Brent, not necessarily a good thing. It depended on one's character.

"Since I couldn't make it to the funeral, I determined to offer my condolences as soon as possible. How fortunate for me to find you out here with Niccolo. My name is Vigo."

"Vigo who?"

His mouth turned down in a mock frown. "I can see Massimo didn't tell you about me."

She couldn't help but chuckle. "I'm sorry."

"Don't tell him I said this, but I'm the nicest Di Rocche in the family."

Something clicked in her memory. "You must be Sansone's son."

His expression brightened. "*Sì*."

"I haven't met him yet."

"I never met your brother. Now that I've seen you, I can understand why Pietra ran away with him."

She could do without his flattery, especially when the mention of Shawn triggered the usual reaction. This time however she was able to prevent her tears from falling. "They were very much in love."

"Believe it or not, I envied them." With that comment she couldn't help but warm to him.

His gaze dropped to the baby sling. By his expression he hadn't seen anything like it before.

"It does look odd, but Nicky likes it," Julie explained. "This way he stays right against me."

He moved to her side to get a better view of the baby, who was still awake. "I would say Niccolo was your *bambino* except for the eyes. They're dark like Pietra's."

"She was a beauty."

"Agreed."

For that remark Julie gave him extra points. "I was just about to take him for a walk into town."

"Permit me to accompany you."

She shook her head. "That's all right."

"You prefer to be alone? I suffered the heavy traffic all the way from Milano to pay my respects."

That, plus his crestfallen look, made up her mind for her.

"If you want to." Massimo had told her to come to him if she felt uncomfortable, but she didn't. Not with Vigo. "I'm going to play tourist for a while. I've never been to Europe. Everything is a new experience."

He smiled. "I've been at university and rarely come to Bellagio. It's been at least three years. We'll explore together."

Vigo turned out to be an entertaining companion. She saw none of the dour traits his uncles exhibited. He bought them ice cream called gelato. After one taste she fell in love with it.

They walked the crowded cobblestone streets and arcaded buildings that gave the town its charm. Used to the hills in San Francisco, she was ready for the steep steps in between the shops. They convinced her a stroller would have been an encumbrance.

Nicky loved being outside. Though not as hot as Sonoma, it was plenty warm. At one point she stopped at a stone bench along the lakeside promenade to give him some water from a bottle she'd packed. He tried to hold the bottle himself and drank thirstily.

Her companion smiled. "Niccolo's got the right idea. Why don't we eat dinner at the restaurant we just passed."

Before she could tell him she had to get Nicky back to the villa, a forbidding male voice said, "Haven't you got studies, Vigo?"

Julie's head flew back to confront Massimo's black look eyeing the three of them intently. Vigo looked startled.

"*Buonasera*, Massimo. It's been a long time." After a tense pause, "I'm sorry about Pietra. I was just telling Julie."

"Were you indeed," came the withering comment.

Vigo cleared his throat nervously. "I came to see you, too, but as she was going for a walk, I invited myself along to get better acquainted with Niccolo." Vigo was putting on a good act, but Julie could tell he was uncomfortable. "I guess I'd better get going."

The encounter had turned ugly. Julie felt she had to say something. "It was very nice meeting you, Vigo. Thank you for the gelato."

"You're welcome."

"Better call your father on the way to your car," Massimo rapped out. "He phoned a while ago, no doubt looking for you."

Vigo looked less than thrilled. He gave him a nod before walking off.

Julie lowered her head because she hadn't seen this side of Massimo since she'd confronted him at the hotel. This was the side she'd been fearing would resurface.

His tone, his whole demeanor bordered on ice. Nicky must have sensed the tension because he'd stopped drinking.

"I'll burp him," Massimo declared. In a lightning move he took the baby from her and put him against his broad shoulder. The next thing she knew he threw up his water and part of his earlier formula.

"Oh, no!" she cried.

It ran all over the open-necked blue sport shirt that complemented Massimo's burnished complexion. Maybe Nicky's tummy upset frightened him because he started crying so hard, people were looking at them as if they'd done something terrible to him.

"Here." Julie pulled out a cloth and would have wiped off his shoulder, but he told her to put it back. "We need to get him to the villa fast. He looks flushed."

She put her hand on the baby's forehead. He definitely felt feverish. Massimo was right. This wasn't like Nicky.

Riddled with guilt, she gathered the sling, then had to run to keep up with him. "I must have kept him out too long, but it doesn't feel that hot."

"Maybe it's the change in climate." He pulled the cell phone from his rear pocket without missing a stride. "I'll call Lia to send for Pietra's physician. She'll have Dr. Brazzi's number."

Following his brief conversation spoken in rapid Italian, they accomplished the walk in record time with Nicky crying all the way. When she noticed Vigo's car was gone, she shivered in relief.

Massimo took the stairs two at a time to the nursery. After changing the baby's diaper, he walked the floor with him whispering endearments like any anxious, devoted father. She saw no hesitation in his movements. No second-guessing. He did what came instinctively.

Minutes later Nicky laid his golden head against Massimo's neck. His cries had become whimpers. In front of her eyes Julie watched them bond.

A lump swelled in her throat to see his little body nestle

closer to his uncle, whose wavy black hair provided such a contrast. Nicky had just discovered security in a pair of masculine arms other than his father's.

Soon Julie heard sounds behind her. When she turned, she discovered Lia had come in the room with a short, middle-aged woman carrying a doctor's bag. She greeted Massimo warmly, then turned to Julie. After introductions were made, she took the baby from him. Immediately he started crying again.

Julie moved to the end of the crib to watch her take his vital signs. Her heart pounded in fear that something serious might be wrong. Massimo stood next to the doctor, his striking features taut with concern.

While the doctor listened to his lungs, Massimo flashed Julie a glance she didn't dare examine too closely. He'd been angry earlier. Now this crisis.

"Several things could be responsible for his spike in temperature," the doctor said, breaking in on Julie's torturous thoughts. "He could be teething early or he could be coming down with a summer cold. There's a third possibility.

"Because his fever came on so fast, he could be developing a condition called rosiola, which is very common with infants. They're grumpy and off their food for a day or two. Watch for a rash."

"He has one already," Massimo said before Julie could.

"No, no. This one will cover his trunk and face. But whatever is wrong, it's not serious."

"Thank heaven," Julie cried. Again Massimo eyed her; however, this time relief dominated his expression.

"In all three instances, the treatment is the same. Give him the liquid baby ibuprofen."

"I brought what Pietra used for him."

"Good. Follow the directions. Keep him hydrated. If he

doesn't want his formula, coax him first with a little sugar water. It's an old trick, but it works better than a lot of the products on the market."

She closed her bag. "Call me if you have any questions."

"We will," Massimo asserted.

Julie shook her hand. "Thank you so much for coming."

"My pleasure. Pietra was a lovely woman. He's a lovely baby. What a tragedy his parents are gone. He's going to need all the love you can give him. That'll get him better in a hurry."

Tears glazed Julie's eyes. "We know."

While Massimo walked her out of the room, Julie reached for Nicky. "I'm going to give you some medicine, then warm you another bottle of formula. We'll take it slowly until you're all better."

Three days later the rash came, signifying that the worst of the rosiola was over. Massimo had taken turns with her getting up with him in the night. During the daylight hours they'd continued to spell each other off.

She'd thought he might leave for Milan to start working, but he stayed home with her. If she hadn't known better, she'd have thought he was the father.

Thankfully Nicky was taking his formula again. On the fifth day she walked in just as he was making noises to get attention.

"Good morning, you cute little thing." Julie pulled the baby from his crib to give him a bath.

In a minute she'd filled the sink with warm water and had removed his sleeper and wet diaper. "You don't have any idea how adorable you are. Your auntie loves you so much." Before she picked him up, she couldn't resist kissing his little cheek and neck.

"This looks fun. Can anyone join in?" sounded a familiar male voice full of life.

Massimo— His vital presence behind her set her pulse tripping. He must have just come from the shower. She could smell the soap he'd used. At a glance she saw he was casually dressed in shorts and a T-shirt like she was wearing.

"Wh-why don't you bathe him," she said on impulse. "He'd love it, wouldn't you, Nicky?"

"If you trust me. This will be another of many firsts," sounded the deep-timbred voice.

Their eyes met briefly before she looked away.

"Through trial and error I've discovered you really can't do it wrong. This is his favorite part of the day. Just lower him gently into the water."

With painstaking care Massimo followed her advice. Soon the bathroom rang with his rich laughter as Nicky kicked and splashed, soaking them both. He got so worked up, every inch of his body shook with excitement. The little noises he made sounded like he was trying to talk.

Julie poured a drop of baby shampoo on his head. Massimo rubbed it in, making a lather before carefully rinsing off the bubbles. They worked in harmony. After she dried Nicky off, he applied the baby powder and fastened a clean diaper. Then she put him in a little stretchy suit.

"That's our big boy," she said without thinking. Hopefully Massimo understood what she meant. "I-if you'll hold him, I'll clean his ears." She reached for a cotton swab. "This is the only part he doesn't like."

While the baby fought her, she felt Massimo's low chuckle to the marrow of her bones. "There!" She kissed the top of his head. "We're all done."

Massimo lifted him in the air. All the way to the bedroom

he kissed his tummy the way Shawn used to do. The baby was all smiles. Julie could tell he loved his uncle's attention.

She had to clear her throat to remove the lump. "I'll get his bottle."

"I already asked Gina to bring it along with our breakfast," he explained.

He thought of everything, yet any more togetherness and it was going to feel as if they were a family, which they were in a sense. But they really weren't!

This was borne out when the maid, who was probably in her early twenties, came in with a tray and a bottle. Julie noticed right away how the other woman's curious gaze darted back and forth between her and Massimo before she left the nursery.

If you didn't know better, you could misconstrue what was going on. A younger nanny in residence with a husband and wife was one thing, but this was a bachelor's domicile.

Ages ago Pietra had made it clear that her brother would never marry. She hadn't explained why, and Julie hadn't pried because at that point in time she hadn't met Massimo and wasn't consumed by curiosity the way she was now.

A man like him would never marry a woman unless it was his choice, so whatever had put him off the institution, the reason went much deeper than his desire to thwart his uncle. And she mustn't forget that getting involved with Massimo would be a mistake.

Not wanting to break up the happy twosome, Julie reached for the bottle. "You'd better be the one to feed him. Nicky's so engrossed with you, I think I'm jealous again." She'd said it with a smile.

But when she handed it to him, his startling black gaze pinned hers. "If this were a competition, I would have been dead in the water long before now. For someone who isn't a mother, you could fool me."

Coming from Massimo, it was the supreme compliment. "Nicky's easy to love. Do you see a lot of Pietra in him?"

"Some. Oddly enough I see more of you."

Her heart did a kick. "It's the blond hair."

"It's something more. An expression he gets when he wants something. I've seen that same look on your face."

"Hunger pains you mean?"

He burst into laughter, transforming him into the most handsome man she'd ever seen or known. Terrified of her feelings, which were growing more and more intense, she reached for the thermometer to take Nicky's temperature.

"It's still normal."

"Better yet, his rash is gone. Mine took considerably longer to go away."

Her head swung around in his direction. "I don't understand."

"At the time Nicky was born, I was bitten by a mosquito that gave me dengue fever."

The breath froze in her lungs. It sounded hideous whatever it was. "Wh-what did it do to you?"

"Laid me up for months, gave me a rash. Luckily it wasn't the hemorrhagic type."

She moaned. "Were you in a hospital all that time?"

"Not all, no."

When she recalled all the terrible things she'd said to him, she was mortified. Her fingers curled so tightly around the crib railing, it cut off the blood supply.

"How come you didn't tell Pietra?" she whispered.

"Because she was so happy with their new baby. I knew my news would worry them unnecessarily. After explaining that the group needed me, I promised to spend the entire month of September with them so I could get to know my nephew."

A promise he would end up keeping for a lifetime.

Moistening her lips nervously she said, "Is dengue fever like malaria?"

"You mean does it keep coming back?"

She nodded.

"Not in my case."

Thank God.

"Happily Nicky has recovered from his rosiola much faster, and is all better now. That's one crisis averted."

One?

Though his words revealed satisfaction, his eyes held a disturbing glint. She noticed he rubbed the back of his neck in what seemed like a weary gesture. But the action indicated there was something else on his mind.

"Now that he's asleep, we need to talk."

Julie knew what was coming. It had only been a matter of time. "I-if you're upset with me for taking him out the other day without checking with you first, I promise it won't happen again."

"I had no problem with your leaving the villa," he replied calmly. "You told Gina. That was the important thing."

"Yes, but she wanted to wake you and I told her not to. You looked so exhausted before you went to bed, I didn't want anything to disturb you."

"I appreciate your concern."

His gaze wandered over her upturned features, but she couldn't tell what he was thinking. It made her nervous, causing her mind to jump to the other possibility that might have upset him.

"In case you were wondering, Vigo invited himself along."

"It would be shocking if he hadn't," came the mocking aside.

Not knowing how to take that remark, she looked away, rubbing her damp palms against the sides of her jeans.

"I know you told me to come to you if anyone in your family made me nervous, but he seemed harmless. I was afraid saying no to him would come off sounding rude."

After a pause he asked something totally unexpected. "Did you enjoy his company?"

"He was entertaining."

"What did you discuss?"

She eyed him warily. "He told me about his life at university. Massimo—what's wrong?"

"Seeing the two of you together reminded me that your decision to help take care of Nicky is depriving you of a full life."

"Nicky *is* my life—" she blurted out.

He shifted his weight, making her aware of his compelling masculinity. "I agree he's the focus right now, but in another week he'll be used to his home here. You'll be able to leave."

Leave?

So he *had* told Dante she was only here for a visit.

Heat swarmed her cheeks. She was too angry for tears. Was this how he'd planned to exact his revenge?

"I realize we didn't have a definite time in mind when you no longer needed my help, but I was thinking a year at least—"

"That's out of the question." He was sounding like her mother.

"Two or three weeks with him is no time at all!"

"It's enough to get him over this first hump. Any more time will only make the separation harder for...everyone."

Julie had an idea the beautiful woman who'd met Massimo at the airport was the reason for this ultimatum. Seraphina must have told him he didn't need a nanny for Nicky, not when she was there for him in any capacity he wanted.

The vision of the two of them entwined still had the power to destroy Julie.

Though dying of the hurt, she used every bit of control she could muster not to rage in front of him. She'd done that once before and had lived in a constant state of anxiety ever since.

"You're right," she admitted with reluctance. She would miss Nicky so much. How could she leave him? "If you feel that strongly about it, I should probably leave by the weekend."

"That decision is entirely up to you."

Thanks a lot.

Almost choking with pain she said, "It's clear to me I should never have come to your hotel. I said some outrageous things and put you in an impossible position."

His jaw hardened. "Up to now Nicky has needed both of us."

Up to now…

"He needs a permanent stable home. You've given him one, Massimo." What could she do? After pressing her lips together she said, "Thank you for letting me come with you while you settled him in."

Almost through the door she heard, "I'm the one who's been grateful, particularly knowing you postponed your marriage plans to help me with Niccolo."

Marriage plans—

Julie wheeled around and stalked back into the nursery.

"What are you talking about?"

He looked at her through veiled eyes. "The reason I went looking for you in town the other day was to tell you your fiancé had called the villa. But when Nicky became ill, everything went out of my head."

Her body shook with anger. "Brent talked to *you*?"

"To Lia. She conveyed the message to me. I assumed by now he'd reached you on your cell phone."

"Let's get something straight." She threw her head back. "For reasons I don't want to go into, I didn't bring my cell with me." That way she could control the talks with her mother. "Furthermore and most important, there were no wedding plans. There was no official engagement. I don't have a fiancé."

Massimo's hands went to his hips. "He seems to think otherwise."

"He lied. Brent lacked certain traits that killed my feelings for him, but he has a big ego. When I told him it was over, I dented his pride and little else. No doubt he got the number of the villa from my father. Hopefully by now he realizes I'm not going to call him back."

"You're telling me the truth?"

Without considering the wisdom of it she said, "I guess if you told me Seraphina wasn't *your* fiancée, I wouldn't believe you, either."

"*Touché*," he muttered after a brief silence.

She heaved a frustrated sigh. "At the time Pietra told you I was involved with Brent, I thought there could be a future with him. But over the last few months I discovered a selfish streak in his nature. It all came to a head when I told him I was going to quit my job to take care of Nicky."

Massimo moved closer to her. "I'm assuming he didn't want to share you."

"A man in the fast lane on his way to the top doesn't always see what's more important." Brent wasn't like Massimo. No man was.

She stared at the gorgeous male confronting her. "Before you tell me there's still time to get my old job back, don't! If I'd wanted it that badly, I wouldn't have approached you. Everyone thinks they know what's best for me. My mother, my brother, my boss, Brent, even you seem to have my future all planned out, but I have news for you. You don't!" Her voice throbbed. "If you bothered to ask, I'd tell you Nicky is what's best for me. I'm best for him, too. He's my nephew as much as yours. No matter what happens, I'm not going to stop loving him.

"You said our family could come often and stay as long as we wanted. Well, I'm staying, even if Dante told me good riddance."

Massimo's expression turned black as a thunderhead. "When did Dante speak to you?" he demanded.

She bowed her head, wishing she hadn't said anything.

"Tell me or I'll get the truth of out of him myself!"

"No, Massimo—" Her head flew back. "It was just something he said as we were getting off the plane in Milan."

"Go on." He stood there with his hands on his hips in an aggressively male stance that prevented her from thinking clearly.

"He told me to have fun on my vacation."

Some choice Italian invective escaped his lips. His reaction made her realize Dante's remarks had angered him more than she would have supposed. She wished she could take comfort in the fact. But the truth remained that Massimo wanted her to leave.

Cut to the quick, she made it as far as the hall before masculine hands closed over her upper arms. He dragged her quivering frame into his chest where she felt a strong heart pounding against her back.

"I meant no offense, Julie," he murmured in a thick-toned voice. "Don't you understand I was only thinking of your happiness with Brent when I suggested your leaving? Nicky needs you. Anyone can see that."

Her emotions were so chaotic right now, she couldn't think while she was clamped to his hard body. He smelled of his own masculine scent and Nicky's baby powder. His warmth, his lips in her hair, everything was an assault on her senses if he'd but known it.

"I need him."

"You think I'm not aware of that?" Massimo whirled her around, his eyes blazing. "If you have any question in that regard, then you don't know me at all," he ground out. "No matter what happens, we're in this together now."

After being plunged to the depths, his words had just given her heart the workout of its life. Out of breath, she stared into his fiery black depths.

"A woman important to you might not like the arrangement, even if you and I are related through Nicky."

He inhaled sharply. "You're referring to Seraphina."

"If she's the important woman in your life, then yes."

His hands trailed down her arms until he let go of her. The loss of contact caused Julie to moan inwardly. She stepped away, afraid to get that close to him again for fear he'd sense how much she desired him.

He folded his arms across his broad chest. "There was a time when we were intimate." Julie knew it. "But that was over three years ago, long before I left for Guatemala."

"From the look of it, she still wants you. I thought she

must have said something about me, and that's why you brought up the subject of my leaving."

Their eyes met. "It appears we've both made erroneous assumptions. However, with you in residence, she might finally get the message."

Julie smoothed the hair off her temple. "So now I can serve another purpose and be a buffer between the two of you?"

His body stiffened. "I'm going to pretend I never heard that."

"Sorry," she whispered before looking away.

"It's my fault for frightening you about the inner workings of the Di Rocches."

"Do you include Vigo under that umbrella? He acted terrified when you caught up to us. Is he like the others underneath?"

"Probably. I wouldn't put it past Sansone to have sent his son on a hunting expedition."

Her head came up. "In search of what?"

"To learn my plans. That way he can launch an offensive before I step foot in the office."

"He's that ambitious?"

Massimo rubbed his bottom lip with his thumb. "Sansone intends to be the head of Di Rocche's one day."

"He's afraid of you. Why? He's the first-born son."

"Of Uncle Aldo, yes. He's been in competition with me since I was born. When Pietra and I had to move to Milan to live with our uncle, Sansone couldn't stand for his father to show us any attention."

"But he's ten years older—"

"That gave him an advantage, one he's never failed to let his brothers or me and Pietra forget."

"But how could he have possibly felt threatened?"

He gave an unconscious shrug of his powerful shoulders.

She shivered, knowing there was a lot more to it than he was letting on. "For what it's worth, Vigo didn't ask me one question about you."

He flashed her an ironic smile. "He has eyes in his head. Like any normal male, he responds to a beautiful woman."

"Be serious, Massimo."

"You think I'm not?" he challenged.

Julie would love to believe him, but she didn't dare read too much into it.

"Vigo was fun."

"I'll admit he's still wet behind the ears. Maybe there's hope for him yet." Beneath his words Julie sensed he didn't believe it.

She and Vigo were close in age. That probably meant Massimo didn't consider her completely grown-up yet. Julie would do well to remember that so she wouldn't make a fool of herself.

So far she was batting a thousand in that department. Every accusation she'd thrown at him was turning out to be unjustified.

"Since I'm back to being in your employ again, I'd better check on Nicky."

His dark brows knit together. "I don't like the idea of you considering yourself the hired help."

Julie wasn't particularly fond of it, either.

"I have an even stronger aversion to the appelation 'nanny.' Naturally I'll go on paying you, but I prefer to think of you as a member of the family who has come to be with our nephew at my invitation. *Capisci*?"

The Italian word had slipped out. It was one she recognized. Her pulse beat a swift tattoo.

"Yes."

"*Bene*. This evening when it's cooler, we'll take Nicky out to dinner with us. We've been trapped in the villa too long. Plan to wear something semidressy. It's time the two of you were introduced to his Italian roots."

Massimo had been away several years. He would have to be inhuman not to want to explore his own backyard again. Despite his extended family's machinations, there had to be certain memories from his youth that were precious to him. She was already counting the minutes.

CHAPTER FIVE

JULIE leaned against the ferry railing. A warm breeze tangled the hair she'd left loose from a side part. Occasional wafts molded the skirt of her lightweight plum-colored dress against her legs. Massimo stood next to her holding the baby, who was wearing an infant life preserver.

"Do you see that hotel ahead of us, Niccolino?"

She smiled. Niccolino?

Massimo was showing the telltale signs of being crazy about the baby he'd nurtured during their all-night vigils.

"When your mama and I were very good, your grandparents used to bring us here for dinner."

Nothing delighted her more than to listen to him talk to their nephew, who was watching him in fascination rather than taking in the fantastic view. How she envied the baby.

Julie had to force herself not to stare at his uncle. This evening he wore black trousers and a silky black shirt. The combination of black hair and eyes with his tanned skin made him so striking, every female tourist gazed unabashedly at him.

According to Massimo they were headed toward the little lakeside resort of Cadenabbia ten minutes across the water from Bellagio. The steep hillsides covered in heavy foliage provided an enchanting foil for the sheltered village below. In case Nicky grew too tired, they could be home in less than a half hour.

The Riviera Ristorante appeared to be a long-standing, family-owned establishment. The minute they stepped inside the doors, a stout older man hurried through the crowd to greet them wearing a broad smile on his face.

"Massimo." He clapped him on the shoulder before breaking into a lengthy spate of Italian. His eyes kept darting to Julie and the baby.

"Leo?" Massimo broke in at last. "Niccolo is Pietra's child, not mine. Signorina Marchant is his aunt."

"Ah… Forgive me for thinking you were the proud parents. I thought of course you'd returned to Italy with your beautiful new American wife and baby."

Her blond hair made her a marked woman. Every time the three of them ventured out in public, people were going to believe she and Massimo were married.

"Where is Pietra? I haven't seen her for a long time."

While Massimo explained, Julie lowered her head. Maybe one day it wouldn't be so painful. That time couldn't come soon enough for her.

The owner appeared visibly saddened by the news.

"Do you have infant seats?" she eventually asked. For all their sakes she wanted to change the subject.

"*Certamente.*" He snapped his fingers at a waiter before showing them to a table on the terrace overlooking the water. Within seconds the other man appeared with a high chair on wheels. He placed it at the end of the table.

Still holding Nicky, Massimo helped her into her seat before settling the baby securely. To her relief he seemed to like what was happening. First he patted his hands on the wooden tray. Then he tried to sit up straight. His blond head bobbed while he took in his surroundings like any grown-up.

"Look who's in charge," Massimo quipped with a distinct note of pride in his deep voice. Julie chuckled because she'd just been thinking the same thing.

As he sat opposite her, she could feel the eyes of the waiter and patrons observing them. Like the owner, they assumed the three of them were a family out together for an enjoyable evening.

Julie was in danger of wishing it were true.

"Do you trust me to order for us?"

She cast Massimo a covert glance. "Since I can't read Italian, maybe you'd better."

"Any allergies to seafood?"

"None."

"Then you're in for a treat."

While he talked to the waiter, she reached in her purse for one of Nicky's plastic rattles and put it on the tray. Pretty soon the baby felt for it with surprising dexterity and tried to bite it.

"Everything goes in his mouth," Massimo remarked once they were alone again.

"I've noticed that, too. Maybe the doctor was right about him teething. I've heard it can be painful."

"Let's not assume anything yet. I've hardly recovered from this latest crisis," he drawled.

"I know. It feels good not to be worried sick about him for a little while." She sat back in her seat with a sigh. "Thank you for suggesting we eat dinner out. Every time I look around, I see a sight more enchanting than the one before."

"That's why I brought you here. This is the best spot to see Bellagio."

"It's too breathtaking to be real. I know I keep saying it, but it's true."

"Twilight tends to bring out her natural beauty."

Though they'd been talking about his birthplace, his dark eyes were centered on her. Deep in her core a trickle of heat grew and intensified until it filled her whole body.

Just then Nicky's hand brushed the toy off the tray on her side. She reached for it, thankful for the distraction in order to get a grip on her emotions. For a moment there she wanted to believe Massimo was actually seeing her as something more than the baby's aunt. What an idiot she was.

As she started to sit up, she noticed the thin spaghetti straps of her dress had fallen below her left shoulder. Someone else noticed, too. Blushing furiously she pulled them back up, hoping he realized she hadn't purposely tried to draw his attention.

The only way to recover was to avoid his eyes while she kept Nicky entertained throughout dinner. Her polenta and scallops were delicious, but she refused the wine and kept waiting for the meal to end. She didn't mind that the baby finally grew restless.

"I think we'd better get him home." She plucked him out of the high chair before Massimo thought of it, conscious that the atmosphere between them had altered. She lamented the fact that she couldn't be alone with this man without being physically aware of him.

"You don't want dessert first?" he asked suavely. His eyes played about her mouth.

"No, thank you. You go ahead and eat while I take Nicky for a little walk."

"A walk sounds like a good idea." He pushed himself

away from the table and stood up. Leaving several large bills, he escorted her toward the entrance.

Why was it that an impersonal gesture like his hand cupping her elbow disturbed her in a way that sent sparks of longing through her nervous system? She'd be surprised if he couldn't feel them shooting around like fireworks beneath her sensitized skin.

It was dark by the time they reached the villa an hour later. Lia met them in the foyer. Another rapid conversation in Italian ensued.

Julie finally dared to raise her eyes to him. "Is there anything wrong?"

"Nothing serious. My uncle's been trying to reach me all evening." His eyes glinted mysteriously. "I pulled your trick and didn't take my cell phone with me."

"In that case I'll put Nicky to bed so you're free to call him back."

Without waiting for his response she rushed up the stairs clutching the baby to her. This was the reprieve she needed to give herself time to deal with her feelings.

They were running all over the place.

While Massimo half listened to his uncle's concerns about the employees he'd had to let go because of the drop in company profits, he paced the floor of his study anxious to get off the phone. He was needed upstairs.

"Since your arrival home, no one has seen hide nor hair of you. How long does the aunt intend to stay?"

His stomach clenched unpleasantly. The aunt?

He'd been waiting for his uncle to get around to the real point of this conversation. Thanks to his cousins, who would have alerted their father from California, Julie's presence in the villa was no secret. It had to be eating at his uncle.

Therein lay the crux of Massimo's growing turmoil. He'd put one problem to bed today. They'd agreed she would stay on because she was family, period. Yet the fact remained he hadn't eliminated the personal threat to his peace of mind. Anything but.

"Vigo says she's very attached to the baby."

Massimo had told Julie that Vigo had been sent to spy. This confirmed it. Nothing had changed during his two-year absence.

"Considering how close she was with her brother, that's only natural."

"It wouldn't be wise to let this go on."

For Massimo's own private reasons he agreed with his uncle. Over the past week he'd been at war with himself where she was concerned. Shawn had referred to her as his baby sister.

In truth she *was* young, yet he had to admit, albeit grudgingly, she was no baby. Furthermore Julie was his brother-in-law's sister, a fact that placed her squarely outside the category of women he normally associated with. Though she was Nicky's aunt and he adored her, Massimo realized the situation couldn't continue like this indefinitely.

But when he reflected on their evening and the way she was able to make their nephew smile, the thought of putting an end to it made his teeth clench.

"The baby needs her right now."

"Granted, he needs a woman to take care of him. But see here, Massimo—if there were no sister, this would be a moot point. Get rid of her. Every day that passes since Seraphina met you at the airport, she suffers a little more."

Anger roiled up inside him. "Are you saying she'd like to be Niccolo's nursemaid?"

"You know exactly what I'm saying."

"I'm afraid I don't. Any relationship I had with her has been over for a long time."

"Not on her part, so you know what you have to do."

His uncle lived in denial. "Impossible."

"Mark my words, Massimo—for Pietra's unmarried sister-in-law to stay under your roof any longer will create a scandal you can't afford, and you know damn well what I mean."

Unfortunately, he did know. Any unpleasant echoes from the past, Massimo preferred to leave there.

"Vigo's already smitten with her. You can't have a female like that living with you! Sansone has enough problems with him as it is."

The mention of Sansone in the same breath with Julie raised his hackles. "I'm afraid you've lost me."

"*Basta*—let's not play games. You know I've been waiting for you to come home so I could name you the new CEO."

He knew.

"Have you forgotten I'm Niccolo's guardian?" Massimo questioned in a quiet voice. "That trumps all other consid-erations including filling your shoes. You need to be thinking of someone else like Vercelli. I'll take his place."

"You're needed elsewhere!" he bellowed. "There's no one else but you who can run everything and you know it. None of my sons has your head for business. You inherited my brother's vision."

"I have my sister's baby to raise."

"Fine. Send his aunt packing and marry Seraphina. She'll take care of him while you delegate at your discretion. As long as you're the head of the company, I can die happy."

"You're too young to be thinking about dying, Uncle. Too much hard work has been your enemy."

"I did it for the honor of my parents and their parents. I did it for my own children and for you and Pietra. I refused to let my brother down."

Massimo hadn't seen that one coming. It caught him smack in the gut where his guilt thrived.

"Then you understand how I feel. Niccolo has lost both his parents. I plan to be around in my old age to play with his children." His nephew deserved that much after the tragic hand life had dealt him.

"You want children? Seraphina will give you all you want."

"Niccolo is quite enough."

There was a long pause before his uncle changed tactics. "How long does an old man have to wait to meet Pietra's boy?"

"The baby's been sick."

"So when is he going to be better?"

Massimo closed his eyes. "I'll bring him by tomorrow afternoon at four for a very short visit." There was no avoiding it. Putting off their reunion would only upset his uncle, who was still under a doctor's care.

"*Bene*. Think of what I've said and we'll talk again tomorrow."

If his uncle but knew it, the discussion was already over.

He hung up, needing something to help him throw off the blackness brought on by their conversation. Without conscious thought he left the study and headed for the nursery.

Massimo found Julie sitting on the bed in Nicky's room feeding him a bottle. They were both wearing different clothes. The baby filled out one of his sleeper suits.

As for Julie, she might have removed that fetching dress

in favor of jeans and a T-shirt, but nothing could erase certain images from his mind.

For a brief moment their eyes met. "Is everything all right?" He heard a trace of anxiety in her voice.

Julie had asked a perfectly logical question, but to give her an honest answer wasn't possible. He hadn't been the same since she'd come to his hotel in Sonoma begging for the chance to be Nicky's nanny.

He rubbed his chest absently. "My uncle is demanding to see Pietra's baby. We'll visit him tomorrow afternoon."

She bit her lip. "Did he truly dislike your sister?"

"No. But he's possessive. When she moved to the States with Shawn, he took it as a betrayal." The rest of it Julie didn't need to know.

"That's so sad. He and my mother have a lot in common."

He drew in a labored breath. "Pietra needed my support. I should never have left Italy. She and Shawn could have lived here at the villa with me."

"And therefore they wouldn't have had the accident that killed them?" Julie inquired gently. "I've tortured myself using the same faulty logic. If I'd stayed in Sonoma instead of moving to San Francisco, one of them could have used my car that day. Maybe then only one life would have been taken," she said in a heartbroken whisper. "But it serves no purpose to think that way."

He raked a hand through his black hair. "You're right." How did she get so wise?

"Massimo?" Her eyes beseeched him. "Shawn would never live in another man's house, not even if it was his brother-in-law's. He had his own dreams. In that regard, you two are alike. That's probably the reason Pietra was so attracted to him from the start."

"Is that so…"

Her mouth broke into one of those rare, spontaneous smiles. It kept the dark shadows from closing in on him.

"Yes. Whether you believe me or not, she told me she encouraged you to move to Guatemala. According to her you had a fascination for archaeology from an early age and did brilliant field work."

"Pietra was the president of my fan club of one."

Without breaking eye contact, she stood up to burp Nicky. While she patted his back she said, "You've left out the leader of your cheering section."

"Who would that be?"

"Your uncle. She said you were his favorite person."

"He and my father were very close. It's more a case of his wanting me to fill my father's shoes."

"Well, it explains your cousins' jealousy. History's replete with powerful men who loved someone else better than their own children."

Julie understood a lot more than he realized. He watched her carry Nicky over to the crib. "I think he'd better start sleeping in here from now on or he won't want to leave my room."

A wise decision.

Massimo moved closer. As she put the baby down with a kiss, he covered him with the blanket. Now when he examined his nephew's tiny features, he saw a look of Julie mixed in with the inherited traits of Nicky's parents. The tug on his emotions was growing stronger. But he knew he shouldn't get involved with Julie.

"Massimo?" She said his name softly. "If you have something you need to do, I'll stay in here for a while to make sure he's gone to sleep."

He had no intention of going anywhere. The semidarkness lent an intimacy he was loath to give up. "We'll keep him company together."

After a short silence, she commented, "He's so sweet, isn't he?" There were tears in her voice. "I'm devastated to think tha—"

"Don't think," he said. Her warmth, her femininity, everything he'd been trying to block from his mind since he'd met her assailed him. Against his better judgment he pulled her against his chest.

His only thought was to stave off the pain, but as he wrapped his arms around her, the mold of her lovely body caused him to think thoughts he shouldn't be having. Too late he recognized his mistake.

"He's completely helpless, Massimo." She went limp against him. In the next breath she was sobbing quietly against his shoulder.

Making one more attempt to keep things from getting out of control he said, "We're here for him. That's the important thing." It was the best he could come up with, but it wasn't enough. This was the time to put her away from him, but he found he couldn't.

The desire to comfort her drove him to kiss her temple. His lips brushed against several strands of golden hair that had escaped from the shiny mass. Throughout the flight to Italy he'd longed to bury his face in it.

She clung tighter to him. Had she but known, every move of her body lowered his resistance. "We might be looking after him now, but Shawn and Pietra were so happy with their little boy."

Her pain connected with his own. Now it was comfort he needed as his lips drifted down her soft cheek smelling of the fragrance of her hair and skin. His legs were starting to feel heavy as certain feelings came to life he hadn't felt in a long time and should be pushing back.

But with his emotions in shreds, he found himself seeking something he hadn't found yet. No amount of self-persuasion could stop him. His body quickened when he happened on the quivering warmth of her moist mouth.

Then and only then did he realize this was what he'd been aching for. Whether she would have tried to stop him or not, the hunger inside him had built to a feverish pitch overriding caution.

Without conscious thought his hands roamed her back. Drawing her into him, their bodies joined in a sinuous, throbbing line. In his urgency to provoke an answering response, he began kissing her, blindly searching for assuagement.

He heard a low moan before her lips opened and parted for him. She, too, was seeking solace, but the line between comfort and desire had become dangerously blurred. As he drove deeper, he tasted the salt from her tears. It was all a blend he couldn't get enough of.

One kiss didn't seem to satisfy either of them. In a breathless giving and taking, their need turned into another kiss, and another, until he lost count. She couldn't possibly know the kind of effect she was having on him. A fire had been lit. The pain he'd started out with was fast turning into a craving.

She must have felt the burst of hot flame at the same time because she ended their kiss. Not suddenly or abruptly. It was more a slow withdrawal, like a dream you couldn't hold on to.

Massimo could hear his own ragged breathing. Hers sounded totally under control.

He didn't know what he expected, but it wasn't the look

of concern she gave him out of those haunting blue eyes. Her hands reached up and cupped his face, holding him there.

"Don't worry about what went on just now. Not for your sake, because I know you're older and have scars that run too deep. And not for my mine, because I'm younger and don't know who I am yet.

"Obviously we both needed somewhere to go with our grief. Under our particular circumstances, this was probably inevitable. Now that we've bared our souls to each other so to speak, I feel better and hope *you* do."

She'd caught him completely off guard. While he stood there stunned, her eyes grew suspiciously bright.

"I'm sorry for the things I said to you when we first met. My only excuse is that I was out of my mind with pain." She took another quick breath. "Thank you for giving me the opportunity to stay close to my nephew even when Shawn's will deprived me.

"You took me on faith. Do you have any idea what that feels like? You're a good man. Good night."

Rising on tiptoe, she pressed a light kiss to his lips before she moved to the door leading into her bedroom.

"Wait, Julie—" Not only was he shaken by what they'd just shared, he couldn't allow her to go on believing something that wasn't true.

She glanced back at him warily.

"Before you go to bed, you need to know something."

"What is it?"

He sucked in his breath. "Shawn and Pietra would have named you guardian, but they were afraid you'd be battling your mother all over again. To quote your brother, 'I couldn't bear to think of our mother ruining another marriage.'"

The stillness grew louder while he waited for her response.

"Why didn't you tell me that in the beginning?"

Her question had been asked softly, but he heard the pain behind it.

"Because I didn't know you then, and I'd made a promise."

She took a step toward him, close enough he could see her face, which at the moment was devoid of animation.

"After living in such close circumstances, you know me now. Since you've just admitted they would have named me Nicky's guardian, why don't you let me take him back to Sonoma? It would be the best solution for everyone concerned."

The hell it would. Massimo saw black.

"I'm afraid the answer has to be no."

Her gently rounded chin lifted. "Why don't we let a judge decide that. My stepfather may not be in your class of wealth, but he does well and is a top attorney. When I reveal what you just confided, he'll tell me we have a case, if only to gain shared custody. You know, a half a year with you, the other half with me. Think about it."

He remained motionless in the dark after she'd left until he heard the house phone ring. Fearing Nicky would wake up, he moved swiftly to the hall. Lia met him at the top of the stairs.

"Signorina Marchant's mother is calling from Hawaii. She sounds upset."

Massimo ground his teeth. She wasn't the only one.

His first instinct was to tell the housekeeper Julie couldn't be disturbed. It would only be doing her a favor. But on that one-in-a-million chance this was an emergency, he didn't dare disregard it like he'd done Sansone's call to Cancuen.

He'd refused to answer it, only to receive a text message hours later that changed his destiny. Heaven knew he suffered enough guilt on several fronts to handle any more.

"Go ahead and knock on her door. She's not in bed yet."

He didn't trust himself to get anywhere near her.

Hopefully by tomorrow he would have worked out what it was he was feeling.

Right now his thoughts and emotions were in total chaos. It was going to be a damnably long night and there was no antidote.

The maid had just brought Julie a breakfast tray to the nursery. "Is there anything else I can do for you?"

"No, thank you, Gina. This looks delicious." Julie put Nicky on the bed with a plastic toy so she could eat, but after biting into a roll she realized she was too nervous to enjoy food.

After telling Massimo she might sue for shared custody of Nicky, she could only imagine his mood today. If he'd disliked her intensely on the first day they'd met, it was anyone's guess how he would treat her from now on.

It wasn't bravado on her part. She couldn't continue in this situation the way it was. She was too attracted to Massimo. Last night's aberration was still on her mind.

The experience in his arms had kept her awake for hours. It wasn't something she would ever forget—or wanted to, if she were honest with herself.

In order to be close to Nicky without giving herself away, she was going to have to fight for her life the only way she knew how.

While she was grappling with her ragged emotions, he walked into the room looking splendid in a sport shirt and trousers.

"*Buongiorno.*"

Her gaze flicked to his in apprehension, but his expression remained unreadable. "Good morning."

He reached for the baby and kissed him. "How about coming outside with me, Niccolino?"

Julie shot to her feet. "Before you take him, I wanted to tell you that my mother phoned last night."

"Lia told me." His hooded eyes centered on her. "Can I expect to be served with papers before the day is out?"

She took a deep breath, realizing she deserved that salvo. "I shouldn't have said it. I'm afraid it was another knee-jerk reaction to Shawn's will, and I made you the scapegoat. Please forget I said anything.

"What I wanted to tell you is that mother's still grieving and wants to see Nicky. Since my stepfather's court case is going to take at least two months, she has decided to travel without him. Unless it's a problem for you, she would like to come next weekend for a short visit." Julie would make certain her mother didn't outwear her welcome.

Nicky suddenly let out a loud burp that caused both of them to smile.

"If you recall, I told your family they're welcome anytime."

"Then I'll phone her back and tell her it's all right. Thank you."

Still eyeing her, he inquired, "What else is on your mind?" How did he know?

"I-it's about the visit to your uncle today." She was still hoping to get out of it.

"I promise we won't stay long," he answered her unasked question in no uncertain terms. "Though it's cooler here by the lake, August is one of Milan's hottest months so wear something lightweight and comfortable."

Comfortable meaning what exactly?

Remembering his cousin's impeccable form of dress, she decided she'd better come up with an outfit that wouldn't embarrass Massimo in front of his family. Maybe the cinnamon-brown suit she normally wore to work, but it was more suited to San Francisco's climate.

"There's a boutique in Bellagio called Cavelli's that Pietra used to frequent. We have an account there. If you want something summery, you're welcome to go shopping after breakfast while I entertain Niccolo."

"Thank you. I'll take you up on your suggestion." What she'd had in mind wouldn't have begun to measure up. "But I'll pay for my own dress."

CHAPTER SIX

LATER in the day when Julie and Massimo entered the neo-classically designed Di Rocche villa, she thanked him again silently for his forethought.

In the understated elegance of the salon off the foyer, a large crowd of his solemn, beautifully turned-out relatives had gathered. If she hadn't known better, she would have thought everyone was waiting for a photographer to arrive.

While she stood in the doorway next to Massimo holding the baby, every eye had fastened on her. The sleeveless Cavelli original in an eggshell tone had a crew neck set with tiny blue stones. Combined with matching shoes, the outfit was summery, yet classy.

Before they'd left the villa, Massimo had murmured his approval of her dress, filling her with relief.

"All the usual suspects have gathered," he ground out.

Knowing Massimo's uncle had been ill, she was surprised his doctor allowed this many people to assemble. Young and old, both seated and standing, had grouped themselves around the balding man in the wheelchair. In the background she picked out Seraphina talking to an older man.

Julie wasn't surprised Massimo's former lover had been included in this very private family affair to welcome home

Get FREE BOOKS and FREE GIFTS when you play the...

LAS VEGAS GAME

Just scratch off the gold box with a coin. Then check below to see the gifts you get!

YES! I have scratched off the gold box. Please send me my **2 FREE BOOKS** and **2 FREE GIFTS** for which I qualify. I understand that I am under no obligation to purchase any books as explained on the back of this card.

▼ DETACH AND MAIL CARD TODAY! ▼

316 HDL ENWT   **116 HDL ENW5**

FIRST NAME	LAST NAME

ADDRESS

APT.#	CITY

(H-R-03/08)

STATE/PROV.   ZIP/POSTAL CODE

7	7	7	Worth TWO FREE BOOKS plus TWO FREE GIFTS!
🍒	🍒	🍒	Worth TWO FREE BOOKS!
🔔	🔔	♣	TRY AGAIN!

www.eHarlequin.com

Offer limited to one per household and not valid to current subscribers of Harlequin Romance®. All orders subject to approval.

the prodigal son. After what he'd told her about his uncle picking his cousins' brides, she had to assume Seraphina was still his number-one choice for Massimo.

Except for Vigo, who flashed Julie a private greeting from halfway across the room, the others remained less animated. The sheer formality of their lifestyle stifled her.

How hard for a thirteen-year-old boy and little Pietra to have been forced to conform to such an atmosphere. She glanced at Massimo, whose features had taken on a chiseled cast. She wondered if he wasn't having a flashback.

Nicky kept looking around at the dark oil paintings. He leaned so far back he almost fell from her arms, causing her to cry out in surprise. Suddenly the lines in Massimo's handsome face relaxed and he grinned at her. "Let's get this over with before we have to rush him to the hospital."

"And be labeled unfit parents." She'd said the words under her breath without thinking. Hopefully he hadn't heard her, but a rush of heat to her cheeks betrayed her.

They approached his uncle, who had to be talking to his oldest son, Sansone. In profile she saw too many physical similarities to assume anything else.

The older man broke off talking to him and turned his aristocratic head in their direction. At the sight of Massimo, he got to his feet, brushing off hands that would have helped him. He was dressed in a formal pinstripe suit covering his lean frame; Julie could see the familial resemblance.

"Massimo." He held out his arms to embrace his nephew. An underlying tone of affection reached Julie's ears.

Pietra had never said her uncle was a tyrant. Neither had Massimo. In person Aldo di Rocche appeared to be a proud, hardworking business giant who had an obsessive need to hold everyone he loved close to him. Her mother wasn't that different.

"Uncle?" He kissed him on both cheeks before using his considerable size and strength to make him sit back down. "Allow me to present Julie Marchant, Shawn's sister."

Curious brown eyes that had Massimo's piercing quality studied her at some length, focusing on her blond hair before staring at her directly. "It's a terrible tragedy that brings us together, *signorina*."

"Yes." Her voice caught. "I hope you're doing better, Signor Di Rocche."

His eyes flicked to Massimo. A smile broke the thin line of his mouth. "I am now," he said before transferring his gaze to the baby. "Do you think Pietra's boy will let go of you long enough for me have a look at him?"

"Of course. Why don't you hold him."

Julie lifted Nicky and placed him in the old man's arms. She heard a few Italian oohs and ahs from the women. The face of one of the teenage girls lit up. There was something about a baby…

Nicky took one look at his great uncle and huge tears gushed from his eyes. In a heartbeat he started crying his lungs out. He'd fallen apart so fast even Julie was surprised. His body twisted and turned like a slippery eel, straining the seersucker material of his new light-green suit.

"Those are Pietra's eyes, dark as your mother's. He has her spirit."

"You think?" Massimo chuckled before taking the nearly hysterical baby from him.

Once in his uncle's arms, Nicky settled down immediately, hiding his face in Massimo's neck. His sturdy little body shook several times. He knew where to go for comfort.

Julie had gone there herself last night. Although she'd been transformed by the experience, the soft look in Massimo's eyes while he cuddled Nicky proved he'd forgotten all about it. In fact the scene was so poignant, her emotions threatened to overwhelm her.

"Vigo?" his uncle spoke unexpectedly. "Since you've spent time with Signorina Marchant, why don't you introduce her around and show her the garden. Do whatever you young people prefer. I want to speak to my nephew in private."

Unsure what to do, Julie turned to Massimo. "Would you like me to take the baby?"

He kissed the blond head burrowed beneath his hard jaw. "I think we're doing just fine." Through shuttered eyes he shot her a glance. "We'll come and find you when Niccolo's ready to leave."

That was code for it was going to be a short visit. Nothing could have pleased her more.

"In case you need anything, the baby bag's sitting on the damask chair in the foyer." Unable to help herself, she kissed Nicky's little hand. It was resting lovingly against the taupe silk suit jacket covering Massimo's shoulder.

"You're behaving too much like an anxious mother," Vigo whispered teasingly at her side. "We'll make this quick, then get out of here."

Since she had no other choice but to go with him, she was glad he didn't linger over the introductions. To a certain extent Nicky's presence had made a dent in everyone's reserve. Seraphina and her father proved to be cordial.

But once Vigo got her alone, she didn't like the idea of his taking her for a drive.

"Why not? If you've seen one statue garden, you've seen

them all. I'll take you past the Duomo and La Scala, then we'll come back."

Vigo walked her out to the courtyard where a fountain was gushing. From the center of it rose a sensational-looking male statue. Nearby a number of luxury cars had been parked. He helped her into the sports car he'd driven to the villa.

"Even though Milano was bombed during the war, it's more prosperous than ever and there are still many treasures. The way Massimo has kept you secluded so far, you could miss them altogether before your return to the States."

"Do you know something I don't?" she asked after they'd left the grounds. It sounded like someone wanted to get rid of her.

"I know a lot more than anyone gives me credit for," came the mysterious answer. He turned onto the main road, merging with the late-afternoon traffic.

"Meaning what exactly?"

"That certain parties believe you're after Pietra's money."

Julie blinked. "What in heaven's name are you talking about?"

He glanced at her several times while maneuvering the car between lanes. "There's an innocence about you that makes me think you really don't know."

"Know what?"

"About the Rinaldi fortune."

Rinaldi? "The name's not familiar to me."

"That's impossible. Your brother married one. He knew exactly what he was doing."

She frowned. When Shawn had first introduced her to Pietra, her sister-in-law's long Italian name hadn't registered except for the di Rocche on the end.

"I still don't understand."

"Massimo and his sister come from old money through their mother. She was worth more money than my grandfather was, and your brother knew it."

Julie shook her head. This was all news to her. "Even if it were true, what does it have to do with *me*?"

"The family fears that with Shawn no longer a contender, you're the latest opportunist willing to sell your body to Massimo, and your soul to Niccolo, in order to get your hands on the Rinaldi money."

His rudeness appalled her.

As for being the opportunist he painted, the suggestion was so ludicrous she burst into laughter.

He didn't join in. "After seeing for myself how attractive you are, I can understand why my uncles were so terrified. They phoned my father from California to tell him Massimo was bringing you and the baby back to Italy."

By now she'd recovered. "I'm Nicky's aunt—" came her sober response. "I'm here for no other reason than to help make up for the love and care his parents can't give him."

"If you say so, I believe you," he replied with seeming sincerity, but at this point she didn't know what to believe. "Unfortunately there are those, starting with my grandfather, who don't want any complications to prevent Seraphina from filling the role of Massimo's wife."

Thus keeping all the money in the family?

A shudder passed through her body. "Surely that's up to him."

"Yes… that's what has everybody at each other's throats."

Her head jerked around. Massimo had told her to trust no one. Maybe Vigo was lying to get a rise out of her. But which part was the lie?

"Why are you telling me all this?"

"Because I like you, and thought you should be warned."

She was angry. "I don't need a warning. Let's get something straight. I'm not looking for a husband. What Massimo does is none of my business. I hope that's clear enough. Surely you don't need me to tell you he's his own man and does as he pleases."

"Exactly. That's what everyone's afraid of."

"You're speaking in riddles, Vigo. Please take me back."

"If you wish, but we haven't reached the cathedral yet."

She lowered her head. "I'll see it another day."

One taste of Massimo's Machiavellian world was enough to put her off it indefinitely.

They drove back in relative silence. When they entered the courtyard she was surprised to see Massimo outside ready to leave. Somehow she hadn't expected the visit with his uncle to be over this fast.

He walked down the front steps to meet them carrying Nicky and the diaper bag. Julie had been around him long enough to know his brooding countenance meant he was in a dark place. Whatever he and his uncle had talked about, it hadn't been pleasant.

Despite his negative energy, he looked marvelous. Before he reached the car, she drank her fill of the way his tall, well-honed physique filled out his expensive hand-tailored Italian suit.

As for Nicky, he always looked adorable. She'd never been happier to see him, and opened the car door to kiss him. It felt like she'd been away from both of them for weeks!

"Were you a good boy for your uncle?"

"You would have been proud of the way he behaved himself with me," Massimo anwered for him. "All the female relatives wanted a chance to hold him, but to their disappointment, he refused to go to them." His intent gaze swerved to hers. "The whole time you were gone, he was looking for you."

Her heart skipped a beat. Massimo—

"What do you think of Milano so far?" he asked, ignoring Vigo, who'd climbed out the driver's side and was studying the two of them curiously.

"It's a big, beautiful city. However if you want the truth, I prefer Bellagio." She'd said it because that was the way she felt, and because she wanted to irk Vigo, who'd had an agenda undoubtedly set by his father.

Turning to the younger man she said, "Thank you for the quick tour."

He flashed her what another person might have interpreted as a guileless smile. "Anytime."

"*Ciao*, Vigo," Massimo clipped out, letting the younger man know his presence was no longer required. That suited Julie just fine.

The smile receded. "*A presto.*" He walked off.

"It's been a big day," Massimo muttered. "Let's get Nicky back to the villa."

Sensing his impatience to leave, she couldn't wait to go, either. By tacit agreement they walked around the side of the mansion to the waiting helicopter.

Whatever was on his mind, he kept it to himself. She needed to talk to him about Vigo's revelations, but until they landed in Bellagio and could be alone, a discussion wasn't possible.

Once they arrived at the villa, Lia announced she had dinner waiting for them. Julie opted to put Nicky down for a bottle, then she joined Massimo on the veranda. It overlooked a bed of flowers ranging from the deepest pink to the purest white, including every shade in between.

She joined him at the railing. "I've never seen such gorgeous flowers."

"Our mother grew some of the most beautiful camellias in the region. She was one of only ten planters ranked Master Gardener Emeritus."

"How did she get interested?"

"She developed an interest through her family's head gardener. Before her death she'd cultivated over two hundred varieties. They peaked all year long. Once upon a time I helped her." He sounded far away. "After that I had to rely on other gardeners to keep up the grounds."

Massimo suddenly turned his head in her direction. "Shall we eat?"

"Yes." She noticed he'd discarded his suit jacket and tie. His elegant shirtsleeves pushed up to the elbows only enhanced his virility. Julie fought to keep her eyes to herself.

Once the maid had served their entrée and had gone, he gave her the opening she sought. "Are you still of the opinion Vigo is harmless?"

The direct question hadn't been asked lightly. He wanted information for a definite reason. She was anxious to give it to him.

After taking a bite of the delicious veal she said, "I believe certain forces have turned him into a real troublemaker."

"What did he say that convinced you?"

She rested her fork on the plate before glancing at him. "He warned me your uncle had plans for you and Seraphina. Then he told me something I didn't know."

"What was that?"

"Vigo said your mother's maiden name was Rinaldi. I didn't recognize it and told him so, but he didn't believe me."

Her host studied her through hooded eyes. "Go on."

So Massimo wasn't denying it.

"He implied Shawn married Pietra for an inheritance from your mother's side of the family."

She waited, but again no rebuttal.

Starting to feel anxious she said, "I had no idea there was one. Then he made up some outrageous fiction about my going after it. Can you believe it? *Moi*? I laughed at him of course."

"Tell me Vigo's exact words." Massimo practically hissed the demand.

At this juncture Julie had lost her appetite.

"He…he put things a bit more graphically. He said something about selling my body to you and my soul to Nicky in order to get my hands on the Rinaldi fortune."

Before she could take another breath, he threw down his napkin. In the second before he got up from the table, her breath froze to see the fury in his eyes.

To her chagrin he remained quiet so long she got the sinking feeling his outrage might not be on her behalf. Rather he could be angry at Vigo for telling her a little too much.

Was that it? her heart cried in pain.

She needed clarity. "Massimo—there were times on the jet when I wondered if you and your cousins were discussing me. Did their suspicions convince you I came to your hotel room before the funeral with an elaborate plan to get close to you?"

His hands formed fists against his powerful thighs. The gesture was revealing.

"So you do believe it!"

"Julie—" His voice sounded like it had come from a deep, underground cavern.

Her pain was so intense she jumped to her feet unable to stay seated. "That explains why you wanted me to run back home to Brent!" It was all starting to make a sick kind of sense, intensifying her pain.

"I can see how you would be suspicious. Especially when I was willing to break off with him, and live with you and Nicky in the jungle in order to get my hands on all those millions.

"Evidently those moments in your arms was some kind of test to find out how far I'd go to get my hooks into you. When you found out, you had to do something and enlisted your uncle's help.

"Using Sansone's son who appeared benign enough the other day was a *great* way to get things out in the open. Stick me with him and let him do his worst!"

Massimo swore an oath. Though it was in Italian she couldn't have mistaken it for anything else. "Have you finished?" he bit out, reminding her of another scene much like this.

"What do *you* think—"

His black eyes held a fiery glitter. "Welcome to my world. I warned you it was ugly."

"I *hate* your world—"

In anguish she fled the veranda and raced up the stairs to her suite, intending to get as far away from him as possible. But before she could close the door against him, he'd muscled his hard body inside with virtually no effort.

Julie couldn't get enough air. She felt as if she'd just run a marathon. "No—" she cried when he would have reached out to steady her. His hands on her arms would be a reminder of last night. Remembering how they'd caressed her skin shook her to the foundations.

Out of a sense of self-preservation she backed away from him. The movement angered him. He took a step toward her.

"You're wrong about me," he said in a husky tone, "but

tonight isn't the time to get into anything. I can tell you're exhausted."

"Don't patronize me," she countered, wild with pain. "I'm not a child."

His gaze traveled over her, making her limbs turn to mush. "I'm well aware of that fact, as is everyone else in the family. We'll talk in the morning when we both have clear heads."

"I have other plans for tomorrow." They didn't include him.

"I don't think so," he came back in a forbidding tone, almost as if he'd read her mind.

Adrenaline spilled through her body. "What are you going to do? Lock me in my room?"

His wintry smile alarmed her. "If I have to, in order to make you listen."

"To what? More lies? I don't know what the truth is anymore. Everything changed when my father told me Shawn and Pietra had left a will naming you guardian. None of it made sense then. It's been downhill ever since. I want no part of anyone's secrets. Which reminds me, there's something *you* should know."

While he waited to hear what it was, his dark eyes narrowed on her trembling frame.

"When mother leaves Italy, I'll be flying home with her for good." She hadn't thought of it until just now. No doubt her subconscious was telling her she'd be wise to separate herself from him permanently.

"I thought Nicky was your life."

She swallowed hard. "He is. But a child deserves to grow up in a household where there's the least amount of strife. Absenting myself from yours will be the kindest thing I could do for him."

"Nicky needs you," he said baldly. "When he saw you getting out of Vigo's car, he almost leaped from my arms to reach you."

Was that another lie to soften her up? She was so mixed up at this point she couldn't think.

"Would you please go? I'd like to be alone."

He stood too close to her. She could feel his warmth. "We'll eat breakfast at nine, then I'm taking you and Nicky on an outing. Bring your swimming costume. We won't be returning before nightfall."

She shook her head. "I don't want to go anywhere with you."

"Even an accused criminal is given his day in court before the sentence is passed, Julie. You owe me that much. *Buonanotte*," he whispered before leaving her room.

After what had transpired, she slept poorly.

Needing solace, she crept into the nursery before dawn. The baby didn't stir.

A little less than three weeks ago she'd been sitting in a planning meeting at work when her father had phoned with the horrific news. Who would have dreamed the aftermath would have hurtled her and Nicky out of their relatively safe orbit to this far-reaching place where nothing was as it seemed.

But that was only part of her turmoil. If she were honest with herself, she had to admit she'd reacted violently tonight because she was emotionally involved with Massimo.

He was no longer just Pietra's older brother. No matter how hard she tried to fight it, he'd become much more important to her than that. She was nervous to go anywhere with him later in the morning. Her fear that she'd already made a fool of herself in his eyes was too great.

The ugliness Vigo had brought to light had caused her to

doubt herself and Massimo. Last night she'd thrown accusations at him when she had no proof. A mature person wouldn't gave gone to pieces.

No…not a mature person. Rather, a woman who hadn't fallen in love with him.

"Come on, Nicky. Your uncle asked us to meet him in the courtyard at nine. I'm afraid we're late." Knowing she would be facing Massimo in a minute, the combination of fear and excitement already had Julie feeling a complete wreck.

After putting her hair back in a ponytail, she grabbed the baby and the diaper bag. It was loaded with everything she could think of including her bathing suit. Together they left the nursery and descended the stairs to the foyer.

On her way out of the villa she discovered the housekeeper sweeping the porch. "Enjoy your trip, *signorina.*"

"Thank you, Lia. I hope you enjoy your day, too."

The older woman nodded.

She hurried down the side steps, then looked up into a clear blue sky. Massimo hadn't told Julie where they were going, but he'd chosen an ideal day for an outing. The air was warm, but not yet uncomfortably so.

To her surprise she saw a dark, blue sedan pull around the end of the villa with a sun-bronzed Massimo at the wheel. He might be wearing sunglasses, but his black wavy hair was unmistakable.

The car came to a stop. He levered his hard, fit body from the driver's seat, wearing white cargo pants and a burnt-orange sport shirt that was open-necked. In hand-tooled leather sandals he looked carefree and, for lack of a better word to describe this incredible Italian male, fabulous.

Though she couldn't see his eyes, she could feel his gaze on Nicky. Undoubtedly he'd taken in her jeans and the blue-and-white checked blouse partially covering her navy tank top.

He moved toward them. "I'll put Nicky in the car seat."

As he took the baby from her, their arms brushed. While he settled Nicky in the back, she climbed in front with the diaper bag, trying to control her trembling. She'd thought they would be walking the entire time.

After joining her in front, he drove them out to the road. Turning right instead of left, the route took them above Bellagio, giving her a view of Lake Como's Y shape. Then it wound down to a private harbor farther along the shore where half a dozen pleasure crafts were moored.

He parked the car before accompanying her and Nicky the length of the dock to a gleaming white forty-foot cabin cruiser called the *Camelia*. In honor of their mother obviously.

"What a beautiful boat."

"Pietra and I used to enjoy it. When I left for Central America, I had it stored, but now that I'm back, I arranged for it to be serviced and brought around."

Needing to avoid his touch, she stepped inside before he could offer his help.

"We'll keep Nicky in his baby carrier under the canopy. Go ahead and make yourself at home. When you go below, you'll notice the galley stocked with Nicky's formula and everything else we'll need."

Their own world on the water. Outfitted with a bedroom, bathroom, dining area and galley, they wanted for nothing. She rejoined him on deck where he had a life preserver waiting for her to put on. Nicky had already been fitted into one.

He lay there wide-awake. His velvety dark eyes watched

every movement Massimo made. Who said five and a half months was too soon to talk about hero worship—

Julie sat in the seat next to the baby. Massimo undid the ropes, then jumped back on board, taking his place in the captain's seat across from them. From her angle, she had an uninhibited view of his arresting profile. She knew better than to concentrate on him, but she couldn't help it, even if there was a price to pay.

Once he turned on the engine, they reversed away from the pier. He handled the boat with the accustomed ease of having done this many times before. Soon he changed gears and the boat moved forward gathering speed.

As Bellagio receded, she noticed that some of the charming buildings were so clustered together, they looked as if they were leaning over the water. This would be an artist's paradise.

This morning the lake reflected a gorgeous vibrant blue, bordered on all sides by the slopes of the Italian Alps. She found their beauty almost unreal. If she weren't waiting for an explanation from Massimo that might or might not take some of her pain away, she'd be enraptured by her surroundings.

They hadn't been traveling long when she realized they were headed toward a tiny island covered in part by olive trees. They came up on it fast. She was surprised when he cut speed and they idled toward a lonely dock. There didn't seem to be any people around.

She darted him a questioning glance.

"Welcome to the Isola Comacina, the only island on the lake. When I was a child, my mother brought me here two or three times a week."

"Why so often?"

"The place is full of Roman and Byzantine ruins. We

explored everything together." He was staring into the distance. Only then did she realize he'd removed his sunglasses. "Supposedly, this island was once the headquarters of the Comancine masters."

"I've never heard of them."

"Neither had I. I learned they were medieval stoneworkers who gave Lombardy its preeminence in architecture. Their style preceded the Romanesque style."

"So *this* is where you developed your love for archaeology."

"Yes. It was here I met a man who told me these ruins were important, but they couldn't compare to the ruins he'd come across in Mesoamerica. Whole Mayan cities and temples dating back to the third century still lay buried under jungle growth, untouched and waiting to be excavated.

"What he told me that day fostered a hunger in me so great, it took my mind to a different place. I determined that when it was possible, I would go there and discover those sights for myself."

A shiver chased across her skin to hear him speak so passionately. "I take it you found what you were looking for in Guatemala."

"It's everywhere, Julie. Whole remnants of civilizations greater than our own begging to be unearthed. Guatemala's only a drop in the bucket. When I got word about Pietra, I was working at a Mayan site in Cancuen with a spectacular seventy-two-room palace."

She lowered her head. One phone call had changed the world for everyone involved.

"After my sister was born, our mother brought her here, too. It seems fitting that Nicky is with us today. Come with me and I'll show you around."

He was gearing up to tell her something important. She

realized his mother held the key to whatever had gone wrong in the Di Rocche family. If Shawn knew about it, he'd never breathed a word to Julie. That's what was so perplexing and hurtful.

"I'll get the sling pouch for Nicky. We can take turns carrying him."

She hurried below to find the things they'd need from the diaper bag. Some water, an extra diaper plus a couple of bottles of unopened store-bought formula ought to hold them until they returned to the boat.

By the time she went up on deck Massimo had secured the ropes to the pier. She stepped onto the dock and reached for the baby. Massimo flicked her an intense gaze before he handed Nicky over.

She looked away quickly and settled the baby in the sling. Massimo stashed the items she'd brought up into a small backpack. With that accomplished they were off.

Once past the trees, she spotted a church. When she asked about it Massimo said, "It's the Oratorio de San Giovani. We'll visit it after I show you the ruins. At one time eight churches existed here."

"On this minuscule island?"

He nodded his dark head. "And a castle that was destroyed in the 1100s."

While she followed him to a rocky promontory that gave onto a partial view of the lake, her eyes fastened helplessly on his powerful legs. He moved with the stealth and precision of a jungle cat. She could imagine him in Cancuen, cutting his way through tangled green vines.

But right now she sensed an intensity he was giving off as he walked around showing her traces of past civilizations. What little boy full of adventure wouldn't love this place for his backyard! The tender feelings that image engendered caused her throat to swell.

"Did your father ever come with you?"

"When he could, but he worked in Milan, which made it more difficult."

"My father was a workaholic, too."

He shot her a penetrating glance. "At least your parents were married."

CHAPTER SEVEN

JULIE'S breath caught. "You mean—"

"They lived in sin," Massimo muttered with dry irony.

"I wasn't going to say that—" she defended.

He gave an eloquent shrug of his shoulders. "The truth is the truth. Their affair rocked Milanese society and created a scandal that still sends reverberations throughout the family today."

Julie remembered asking him if the pictures Pietra had shown to her were her parents' marriage photos.

She bit her lip. "Many couples don't get married. It's not—"

"The end of the world?" He finished her thought on a caustic note. "Perhaps not today, but back then it wasn't done. Not if you came from a good Catholic family. Especially not if you came from two good Catholic families whose grandfathers had more money than was humanly decent."

Hurt to the core for him, she wanted to comfort him but didn't dare. Instead she lifted a sleeping Nicky onto her shoulder, needing his cuddling warmth.

"My mother was slated to marry my father in order to keep all the money within both families. But she refused to cooperate."

"Sounds like someone else I know," Julie ventured daringly.

His eyes glittered. "You're right about that."

"I don't blame either of you. Unless it's your choice, no one wants to live with the knowledge they've been sold for a price."

"Except, this story has an ironic twist. My father happened to be in love with my mother. When she turned him down, he went on working at Di Rocche's, but he renounced any inheritance he would have received in order to pursue her."

"That must have come as a huge shock," she whispered.

His dark brows raised. "Both families received an even greater one when my mother ended up living with him."

"Then she did love him?" Julie queried.

"Yes."

"Were they happy?"

"As far as I could tell. But my grandfather Rinaldi wouldn't allow my father to come to the villa."

Incredible. "So what did they do?"

"They would meet here."

She blinked. "What do you mean?"

"They were outcasts. This island was their retreat. The only family life Pietra and I knew with our father was here. The rest of the time he lived in Milan, and we lived at the villa in Bellagio with our mother and grandparents.

"If it was a test to show my father he could never expect to live on her inheritance, he passed it."

"Massimo—" She couldn't imagine it. Not any of it.

"When you're a child, you accept the way you live without thinking about it. Our grandfather had more of a presence than our own father, who would arrive on the island like a visiting uncle. Grandfather died of pneumonia six months before our parents were killed in a freak boating accident."

Julie pressed her lips to Nicky's forehead, unable to comprehend that kind of bitterness. "What about your grandmother?"

"She had a nervous breakdown. Today she could have been treated with drugs and lived a normal life, but those were different times. She ended up in a sanitarium. That's when our uncle came for us and we were taken to Milan to live."

"No wonder you feel a sense of obligation to him."

His jaw hardened. "My constant dilemma, since he made certain Pietra and I wanted for nothing. The truth is, he missed my father. From the moment we were moved there, he began grooming me for the business. But if his agenda was to get hold of the Rinaldi fortune, he was thwarted.

"Not only did Pietra run off with an American, my grandfather left all his money and estate to Pietra and any of her progeny."

Julie felt another jab of pain. "And nothing to you?"

Maybe *that* was the reason Pietra had made him Nicky's guardian. She loved her brother so much, Julie could understand why she'd want him to share in her inheritance if a tragedy did occur.

"My grandfather didn't like me. I was too much a reminder of my father, who had the audacity to carry on a lifetime affair with his daughter."

Suddenly something Vigo had said during the drive yesterday came into her mind.

"Massimo—when Vigo started making assumptions about you and me, I told him he was way off base, that I came to help with Nicky and that you were your own man and would do as you pleased. In response he said, 'That's what everyone's afraid of.' At the time I didn't understand what he meant."

"But now it's becoming clear?" He flashed her a sardonic regard. "Your presence has the family worried. It begs the question why I would marry Seraphina when I already have a beautiful young woman living under my roof.

"After all, my mother didn't bother to marry my father. History could be repeating itself. And as long as you're here to help take care of Nicky with my express permission, what's to prevent you from dipping into his funding at will."

The picture he was painting made her ill.

"What Vigo didn't tell you is that my uncle's company has been losing money for the last few years. He's several million dollars in debt to Seraphina's father. I didn't know that until my uncle confided as much to me yesterday."

Julie groaned.

"Knowing Uncle Aldo's situation, the only thing I can do is get back to work and see what can be done to make things start turning a profit for him again."

Julie had no doubt Massimo could move mountains, but she knew how much he must have hated leaving Guatemala. He had a burning inside him no life here in Italy could quench.

"Your uncle demands too much."

"My father would have expected it of me. Needless to say this isn't what Sansone wants."

Had anyone ever worried about what Massimo wanted?

"Is your grandmother still alive?"

"No. She died two years ago. Before her death Pietra and I used to visit her."

"That was about the time you left for Guatemala."

He nodded. "With her passing, I felt the need to get completely away. But as you can see, fate dictated I come back here again."

She stared at him. "Did Shawn know about the money?"

"Not until they made out their will in front of me. Then he heard the whole story from Pietra I'm telling you now.

"She tried to give me her fortune. I told her I didn't want it. She deeded me the villa, anyway, but I didn't know about it until her attorney mailed me the document in Guatemala. Everything else is in trust for Nicky."

"Is your uncle aware of what's happened to the money?" she asked quietly.

"I told him yesterday. It's all there for Nicky to inherit. My job as guardian is to teach him how to use it responsibly and learn from both families' past mistakes."

Every time he opened his mouth, Julie's love and admiration for him grew.

"What did your uncle say to that?"

"What could he say?"

While they'd been talking, the baby had grown restless. Massimo reached for him. "There's more to see, Niccolino. Come on. I've got something interesting to show you."

They walked to a different part of the island where he showed her some old Roman mosaics whose colors were still vivid. Another time and she would have been riveted. But she'd heard too much information today.

Julie had thought her life had been difficult at times, but Massimo's story unveiled like a Greek tragedy. She continued to explore the rest of the ruins with him, but every so often she glanced at him with a terrible ache in her heart for the pain he'd endured.

He eventually came upon a smooth rock where he sat down to give Nicky another bottle. The baby was acting hungry, but it hadn't been that long since he'd eaten.

"I'm surprised he wants another one this soon."

"He must be going through a new growth spurt," Massimo surmised.

"Maybe." But she decided she would call the doctor when they got back to be sure this was normal. She'd happened to watch a documentary on fat babies with Pietra and didn't want that to happen to him.

"Are you still intent on returning to the States with your mother when she comes next week?"

What?

Massimo's head was bent over the baby so she couldn't see his expression. The unexpected question subtly couched in that low velvety voice hit her like a thunderclap.

If he truly didn't want her to leave Italy yet, he wouldn't have brought it up. He was a master at knowing how to achieve his own ends without confrontation. It hurt so terribly she could hardly breathe.

Don't let him know him how devastated you are. Be natural.

"Now more than ever." She sat down on another rock a few feet away. "Not because I don't believe everything you've told me. On the contrary, it wounds me to think how much you and Pietra must have suffered over the judgments and cruelty from others growing up."

"We survived."

"Mock me if you want, but children shouldn't have to survive!" she replied indignantly. "Much as I want to stay with Nicky, I wouldn't dream of being the source of more abuse that your family and people in general will heap on you. Nicky might still be a baby, but he shouldn't have to grow up in such an atmosphere."

"I have no intention of letting that happen."

"That's good because I have to tell you it wasn't the most pleasant experience to be used by Vigo for target pratice. You were right to warn me about your family. He has a brutal aim."

His head reared. "Vigo's role model is one of the best."

"Forgive me for saying this, but I don't know how you put up with your cousins. You deserve a medal." You deserve to have your heart's desire.

She sucked in her breath. "To get back to Nicky—"

"*Sì, signorina?*" he drawled as if he wasn't taking her comments seriously.

"Since I'll be gone soon, I hope it will be all right if I spend as much time with him as possible until then. That should leave you free to start wielding the proverbial machete while you cut away the debris at Di Rocche's."

He flashed her a white smile. "I like that particular metaphor. You've made me homesick. Could it be you're in a hurry for me to get back to work and out of your hair?"

Her cheeks warmed. "I didn't say that. But I would imagine you miss being busy." Heavens, how could he stand it here now…?

"Taking care of Nicky has taught me the meaning of the word."

Julie laughed sadly. "Me, too. It's a different kind of work, isn't it?"

"I enjoy it," he confessed in a low voice.

"So do I. A smile from him makes it all worthwhile."

His gaze roved over her features. "Smiles have a way of doing that."

Yes. One of Massimo's could melt her into a puddle.

She checked her watch. "I don't know about you but I'm hungry for lunch. Let's go back to the boat and I'll fix it. Afterward I'd love it if you showed us the rest of the lake.

"I remember Pietra telling me Como is the place to buy

silk. I'd like to make a stop there and get my father a scarf for a souvenir. Italian men wear them with such flare."

He got up with Nicky and started walking with her. "I've never worn one."

He didn't need one. He didn't need anything. She came close to telling him he was more perfect than the statue of the Roman god she'd seen in his uncle's courtyard dominating the fountain.

After clearing her throat she said, "I don't suppose Indiana Jones ever did, either."

"*Mi scusi*, Massimo—"

He'd just walked in the front door with the baby. "What is it, Lia?"

"When the *signorina* came in a minute ago, she asked me for the *dottore*'s phone number before hurrying upstairs. I didn't think she looked so good. Do you suppose the boat ride made her sick?"

A tight band constricted his lungs. Had she been covering up all afternoon? He'd been so stunned over her intention to go back to California, very little else had registered during the rest of their sightseeing cruise.

"I don't know, but I plan to find out."

"Tell her Signor Walton called to speak to her again."

Signor Walton could go to hell.

"*Grazie*, Lia."

Tightening his hold on Nicky, he moved swiftly up the stairs. The baby needed attention before being put to bed, but first he would check on Julie. If she was ill, she should have told him.

He saw she'd put her purchases and the diaper bag on the bed in the nursery. His alarm grew to realize she hadn't emptied it yet. Normally she was so efficient, Lia complained there was never anything she could do for her or the baby.

"Julie?" He rapped on the connecting door.

"Just a minute," she called to him.

"I'm coming in anyway."

As he charged through the door with Nicky, she jumped off the bed, almost dropping the phone receiver. Her face was all eyes to see him rush in uninvited.

For being out in the sun a good part of the day, she didn't show it. If anything he thought she looked pale.

"What's wrong?" he demanded without preamble.

She put out a hand to silence him before speaking into the phone. He heard a couple of yeses and a thank-you before she hung up.

"Lia said you were sick. Why didn't you tell me?"

Julie shook her head. "I'm sorry if she got the wrong impression. I was calling the doctor about the baby, not me."

Relief caused his body to relax. "Why would you do that? Nothing seems to be wrong with him." He kissed the top of his nephew's sleepy head.

She smiled nervously. "I know that now, but when he drank so much today, I got worried. I'm afraid Dr. Brazzi thinks I'm pretty hopeless in the mothering department."

If Julie only knew, he had nothing but praise for the way she tended to Nicky's needs. Certainly Lia hadn't faulted her for anything, and his housekeeper was a perfectionist.

He cocked his head. "How much longer are you going to keep me in suspense?"

A worried expression broke out on her face. "Promise you won't laugh?"

"I don't know if I can do that," he quipped while his gaze studied the beautiful way nature had put her features and body together. When they'd stopped to swim at the beach near Mezzegra, Nicky hadn't been the only one who couldn't take his eyes off her.

The curves of her figure clad in a lime bikini with white polka dots had caused him to entertain thoughts he shouldn't be having about his little nephew's aunt. To his alarm they flooded his mind. There seemed to be no end to them.

When he thought of her not being here anymore, he was haunted by an indescribable emptiness.

She chuckled, unaware of his growing turmoil. "You're impossible."

"So I've been told on more than one occasion."

"Well, Dr. Brazzi said he's hungry because he should be eating solid foods by now."

The furrow between his brows deepened. "Not pasta alfredo surely."

Her laugh delighted him. Everything she did charmed him. "No. He's supposed to have baby cereal and strained vegetables like squash. She said to start with rice cereal. You add a little formula to it."

He lifted the baby in the air. "Did you hear that, Niccolino? Your parents have been starving you, but you won't hold that against us, will you?"

If she registered his slip of the tongue, her next comment didn't show it. "Vigo tried to feed him gelato the other day. I have to admit his instincts were better than mine."

Massimo held back his own opinion of Vigo. It wasn't fit for tender ears. "Sounds like it's time to buy a high chair." She nodded. "Tell you what. After we put him down, we'll ask Lia to tend him while we go shopping."

"Tonight?"

"No better time."

"That's a good idea. We're low on everything."

He cast her a covert glance. "Lia asked me to tell you your ex-boyfriend phoned the villa earlier. While you call him back, I'll get Nicky ready for bed."

"That's twice he's rung me. Maybe by the third time he'll get the point."

Massimo doubted it, but none of it mattered. For the time being she was living in his villa of her own free will. Possession was still nine-tenths of the law.

Within the hour they'd made their purchases. When they returned, Massimo was loath to let her out of the car. Her feminine profile, the warmth she generated, the confident way she handled things even if she professed uncertainty—all of it had conspired to seduce him.

"I…I hope Nicky didn't wake up while we were gone." He watched her fingers search for the door handle, but he'd set the lock as she found out when she tried to open it.

"If he did, Lia's there. Ever since we arrived from the States she's been waiting to comfort him."

She stirred restlessly. "I didn't realize that."

"It's only natural since she was devoted to Pietra. But that's no one's fault. There's something important I want to discuss with you before we go in."

He felt her edge closer to the door. "It's getting late, Massimo. Can't it wait until tomorrow?" She wouldn't look at him. Now that she didn't have Nicky as a shield, her eyes seemed to have been avoiding him more.

"I'm afraid not."

Her blond head jerked around, causing her ponytail to swish. "If you've changed your mind about letting me drive your car while—"

"I haven't—" he cut in impatiently. "Whenever you want to go somewhere, ask Lia for the key."

"Thank you." He heard her take a quick breath. "You sound cross. I'm not surprised. It's been a long day."

His hand gripped the steering wheel tighter. "Julie—our arrangement isn't working."

She faced the front once more. "We've already established that fact. Just hang on a little longer. You don't want to deal with my mother alone, trust me.

"Once she arrives, she'll see Nicky's in the best of hands with you and Lia. It won't be hard to convince her my job here is done."

"I don't think so."

"What do you mean you don't think so?" Now she was the one sounding cross.

"I'm not going to let you walk away from Nicky. He's too attached to you now."

"You *know* that's not what I want, either," she fired. "So what do you suggest I do? I refuse to stay here and be the cause of another scandal in your family!"

"I have a solution that will solve all our problems." Until now he didn't realize he'd been holding his breath. "It came to me on the boat."

She slowly turned to him. Even in the semidarkness he could see her blue eyes charge with light.

"Does this mean you're going to give me temporary guardianship of Nicky without going through a court battle?" Tears glistened on her lashes. "If so I think you're the most extraordinary, generous man I've ever known."

Dio mio.

"It *is* the perfect solution for now, Massimo. Without me

here, you'll be spared the trauma of trying to raise Nicky in a hostile environment.

"Luckily Dad hasn't put the town house on the market yet. I talked to him the other day. He's thinking of holding on to it as a future investment for Nicky and renting it out. So you see? I can take the baby back to his own home to live.

"Knowing you, I have every confidence you'll be able to fly to Sonoma once a month. The town house has a guest bedroom we'll make yours. Nicky will come to anticipate every visit.

"Later on, when you think he's old enough, he can live with you in Bellagio and I'll visit him. The speculation about you and me staying under the same roof will be just that. Our nephew will learn to enjoy the best of both worlds, which is exactly what Shawn and Pietra wanted for him.

"Who knows?" Her mouth lifted at the corners. "Maybe by then you'll have saved your uncle's company and be able to go back to Guatemala. It wouldn't surprise me one bit if you turn Nicky into an archaeologist. One day he might even decide to use his fortune to fund an entire excavation project.

"I know I've told you this before and you probably hate it, but you are a good man. The best."

On an emotional high she leaned over to kiss his jaw, but Massimo unexpectedly caught her moist cheeks between his hands. The fierce expression on his face shocked her.

"I'm sorry to disappoint you, but that wasn't the solution I had in mind." His voice sounded like the lash of a whip's tongue.

She felt the blood pound in her ears. "I don't understand. I…I thought we'd come to the same conclusion."

"There's a lot you still don't know about me." His warm breath on her lips had become a disturbing sensation she couldn't deal with right now. "Why are you pretending not to know?"

"You mean the *M* word."

"*Sì, signorina.*"

An angry gasp escaped her throat. She pulled away from him. "You're talking the deadly arranged marriage that has been the backbone of the Di Rocche empire for generations?" As her cry reverberated in the car's interior, she noticed his jaw harden.

"You don't know me at all if you think I'd ever consider it!" She braced her back against the car door. "After your uncle's failed attempts to get you to marry Seraphina, you have the gall to think I'd be overjoyed to rush headlong into another Di Rocche disaster waiting to happen."

His eyes became black slits. "Fight me with everything you've got, but you wanted Nicky enough to break up with your boyfriend."

"Not that it's any of your business, but we were already on the verge of disaster before tragedy struck. It was just a matter of time for Brent and me."

"That's a moot point considering Nicky *does* exist," he inserted with maddening logic. "The truth is, you wanted the baby enough to come to a stranger's hotel room and beg to be taken on as a nanny.

"I think Julie Marchant needs him more than she'll ever admit to herself. But you can't have him unless you take me, too."

There was pain, and then there was *pain.*

"We're talking about *you*, right?" she mocked. "Massimo Rinaldi Di Rocche. The nemesis of your cousins' lives.

"The one who escaped the net and got away without any baggage. The rolling stone who gathers no moss. In a word, the man who has refused to be bought at any price, albeit for the best of reasons.

"You're a brilliant human being, Massimo, but all your theories don't add up to marriage for us because it's not an option.

"In your mother's case I can understand why she avoided the institution altogether. At least she had proof your father wanted her for herself and no other reason.

"After growing up in my home and being torn apart by two people who probably shouldn't have taken vows, I'm not eager to make a mistake I'll end up paying for until death. Nicky deserves much better. A happy home with one parent can work. Shawn and Pietra must have thought so, too."

She looked down at her hands. "It's true I love Nicky, but I'll find a way to live without him if that's what's best for him. Like you said, we'll see him on holidays and vacations. When the two of you come for visits, the guest room at the town house will be waiting for you."

"Until death *does* sound like a long time," Massimo inserted, completely ignoring what she'd just said. "The other day you admitted that you'd hoped to stay for at least a year. To silence any fears your parents might have in that department, and to protect Nicky from my family's venom, we'll enter into a twelve-month temporary marriage. That's as long as I'm willing to try building the company's profits for my uncle.

"At the end of that time you and I will reassess our arrangement. I'm thinking it's possible to take Nicky to Guatemala with me much sooner than I'd hoped. You might want out, or you might want to come with us."

The pulse throbbing at her throat almost choked her. "I think you've lost your mind."

His brows formed a black bar. "Maybe, but I know what's best for our nephew. This is a crucial time for him. He needs us both desperately. We can be married after your mother gets here. If you phone your father tonight, he'll have time to make arrangements so he can give you away."

She stared at him with accusing eyes. "We're not in love!"

"We are with Nicky. Your parents will understand and approve."

"I'm not a little girl. I don't care if they approve or not. This is my life!"

His mouth broke into a cruel smile. "You should have thought of that before you came flying to my hotel room with your proposal. Nicky's happiness is in your hands now. So is your parents'."

"What do you mean?"

"Your brother and my sister cheated them out of a wedding. Ours can make up for it."

"While your uncle suffers a worse heart attack," she muttered sarcastically.

"For Nicky's sake we'll risk it."

"No, Massimo," she whispered.

He leaned toward her, causing his hand to graze the tender skin at the back of her neck. Trickles of delight invaded her body.

"Am I talking to the same person who told me no other woman would ever love Nicky as much as you do? As I recall, you said you'd do anything for him.

"I may not be an expert on child rearing, but I can tell he's bonded with us. Now that he's had a taste of your love, you can't take it away without doing serious psychological damage. I don't know about you, but I'm not prepared to live with that guilt."

Stop talking, Massimo. "I wouldn't sleep with you."

"Did I suggest such a thing?"

"You didn't have to. You're a normal, red-blooded Italian male."

"Thank you. I'm glad you noticed."

She'd done more than that. She'd been a participant and would never recover. A shiver ran the length of her spine. "So what will *you* do?"

"A marriage of convenience is the going term for what we're about to enter into."

"It's disgusting," she said under her breath.

"The convenience part allows both parties to follow their desire." He'd spoken without acknowledging she'd said anything.

Her heart felt as if it was being used for a pin cushion. "Provided both parties are discreet of course."

"*Precisamente.*"

She flung her head back. "Do you know how cold-blooded that sounds, not to mention absurd?"

"It gets the job done," he reminded her. "If Nicky could take part in this conversation he'd tell us to go ahead. For that matter, so would Shawn and Pietra."

"My brother thought I was on the verge of marrying Brent."

She felt a little tug on her ponytail. "He knows better now."

Massimo shouldn't have said that. She got a stifling feeling in her chest.

"What other questions can I answer?"

"Where would we get married?"

"The family attends the Chiesa di San Matteo near the Duomo in Milan. All the marriages have taken place there. We'll have a special mass performed."

"God won't approve."

"I think He will. Instead of sacrificing Seraphina at the altar, we'll be doing this for the welfare of a child."

Julie bristled. "You have an answer for everything."

"I try."

She'd folded her arms against her waist. "It's only been three weeks—"

"Long enough for speculation to have already turned ugly. The therapeutic shock of our marriage will set the family on its heels, which is exactly where I want them. Fortunately, at this point the baby is oblivious."

The baby…

This was all for Nicky. Her little sweetheart.

"You can't expect me to make a decision this quickly."

"That's all right. I've been single thirty-four years. Nicky and I can wait one more day to learn our fate."

"One more day—" she cried in frustration.

"In case you need reminding, I hired you to be Nicky's nanny within a half hour of your tearful petition."

Even though what he'd said was blatantly true, the man didn't play fair with her emotions. "A nanny's quite different from a wife."

"In title only," he answered in a mild tone. "Nothing has to change for us privately."

Her face went hot. "I can promise you it won't!"

"Then I have my answer. Shall we put it in writing?"

Her expression turned mutinous. "I haven't agreed to anything yet. Please let me out of the car."

He smiled. "You had only to ask." She heard the click of the lock, indicating she was free to disappear.

"While you check on Nicky, I'll bring everything in. By the way, I'll be leaving for the office early in the morning.

Don't expect me until dinnertime. You can give me your answer then."

"Don't count on it."

That remote look broke out on his hard-boned features. "I've learned to survive by not counting on anything in this life, *signorina*."

Another truth from his lips. It filled her with fresh despair. "Expect my answer to be no."

He shrugged in that elegant Italian way. "Then so be it. You go home to your life, and I'll continue to raise Nicky. After he realizes you're gone for good, he'll have learned his second lesson in survival. A salubrious experience, considering his unique circumstances."

CHAPTER EIGHT

IN TURMOIL, Julie hurried inside the villa. She found Lia in the nursery sitting in a chair next to the crib doing some embroidery. Nicky was sound asleep.

If she went back to the States, this would be the nightly scene, but she wouldn't be part of it. She felt her heart wrench.

The housekeeper saw her and got up. "He didn't cry once," she whispered.

"That's because he knows you love him."

The older woman beamed. "*Buonanotte, signorina.*"

After she left, Julie stood at the crib looking down at Nicky. There *was* another way to solve their problem that didn't condemn Massimo to a marriage he would never have considered three weeks ago. She *could* find a job and a place to live in Bellagio.

By morning she had a plan.

Relieved to hear the helicopter take off, she got herself ready for the day. Since she was going for a job interview, she decided to wear her cinnamon suit. Arranging her hair in a French roll, she hurried into the nursery to get Nicky bathed and dressed.

After tying a bib around his neck, she fed him his first solid meal. He spit out the first few spoonfuls of cereal.

Hilarious. She wiped his chin, then tried again. Finally he figured out he was supposed to swallow and ate everything in the bowl. Julie laughed delightedly.

"You've been so good, do you want to go for a drive? It looks like another beautiful day."

He seemed eager to get out of the high chair. She packed a diaper bag with all the essentials before taking him down to the kitchen. Lia had breakfast ready for her.

"I'm going out for part of the day," she informed the housekeeper after she'd finished eating. "Massimo said you would give me the car keys."

Lia's brow furrowed with concern.

"I'm an excellent driver, Lia. You have to be to live in San Francisco." She pulled three bottles of formula from the fridge.

The older woman spread her palms. "You haven't driven here before."

"Don't worry. I'll handle it."

"It's a new car."

"I've ridden in it. Don't worry."

She didn't look the least bit happy. "I'll tell Guido to bring it around."

Julie thanked her before heading to Massimo's study. Setting Nicky on the floor in his baby carrier, she checked inside the desk drawers until she found a phone directory.

She was looking for wineries. Why not start there. She'd worked for one part-time while she was in high school. Mr. Brunelli still owned it and would give her a good reference.

Ah. There were several. She jotted down the addresses and phone numbers on some note paper. Though she knew very little Italian, she had learned a few words from Shawn and Pietra. Maybe someone would hire her temporarily, especially if they could use her English skills. It was worth a shot.

If that didn't work, she would investigate the software companies in Milan. But they were further afield. She would prefer to stay close to Bellagio.

Once outside, Guido helped fasten Nicky's baby carrier into the base on the backseat of Massimo's luxury sedan. She thanked him, then settled herself behind the wheel. When she turned on the motor, the gas tank indicated a quarter full. If she needed more, she'd buy it after she'd been out on the road for a while.

With a hundred Euro dollars in her purse, and an area map she'd bought during her walk with Vigo, she was ready to go. Once she'd pulled onto the road, she turned right to avoid the town. The next pedestrian she saw, she would ask directions.

She could have enlisted Guido or Lia's help, but she didn't want Massimo's staff to know what she was doing. If she hoped to convince him her plan could work, this required the element of surprise.

It felt good to be on her own with Nicky for a change. She enjoyed the car's powerful engine as they climbed higher. Five people later she came upon a man who showed her on the map how to get to the Fratelli Orfeo winery.

Nicky behaved beautifully while she talked with the manager. He let her know she would have to speak Italian in order to work there. She thanked him for his time and drove on. If she'd dropped Massimo's name, things might have turned out differently, but she wanted to get a job on her own.

Since Nicky needed a bottle, she sat outside with a group of British tourists to feed him. One married couple was doing a bicycle tour of some wineries and gave her directions for two more a little farther away on the same side of the lake. She thanked them and drove on again.

When she came to the first one, to her dismay they couldn't use her either unless she spoke Italian. The last one near Como displayed the Di Rocche logo on the door.

At this point she was desperate to find work and went inside anyway. When they told her she needed to be bilingual, she mentioned that she was Signor Massimo Di Rocche's relative.

The fact that she was holding his nephew made her story more convincing and changed the tenor of things. She was told they would get back to her by tomorrow.

Julie left, convinced the end justified the means. If she could find a job that kept her close to Nicky, she didn't care if she'd dropped Massimo's name in order to tip the scales in her direction.

Encouraged by the progress she'd made, she decided to gas up, eat lunch and then do a little more sightseeing before going home. But she soon discovered all the gas stations were closed until the later afternoon. When she pulled into a self-service with one pump working, she was driving on empty.

You had to pay in five-note Euros. Luckily she had two in her wallet, only enough for about two and a half liters. It looked as if she would have to go straight back to Bellagio. However, before she went anywhere, Nicky was getting fussy and needed a diaper change.

Taking a baby anywhere was a lot of work. Still she managed. Eventually they headed for home. She figured they were about halfway there when a red light appeared on the dashboard.

"Oh no— Something's wrong, but it can't be because we're out of gas."

Saying a silent prayer that they'd make it to the villa, she moved into the right lane in case she had to stop. Several cars passed her. That was fine. The red light meant there was a problem, so she wasn't taking any chances with Massimo's beautiful new sedan.

Suddenly the car stopped on her. There was no sound of a low battery. Nothing. It just stopped, like it was dead. Her heart plunged to her feet for fear someone would crash into the back and injure Nicky.

Thankfully no one was directly behind her.

Frantic with concern she turned on the hazard lights and jumped out of the car to get the baby. Without a cell phone she would have to walk off road for help.

She'd gone maybe three hundred yards carrying Nicky in his baby carrier when a small car pulled over. A man called to her through the open passenger window.

"*Signora*—" He made motions for her to get in his car but she shook her head.

"Can you call the police for me? Police!"

Nicky wasn't used to her using such a loud voice and he started crying.

"It's okay, sweetheart." She leaned over to kiss his cheek. To her dismay he just cried harder.

The man shouted something back, but with Nicky so upset, she couldn't understand him. The stranger finally drove off.

She probably should have accepted a ride, but she was afraid to trust him. "We'll find someone to help us," she muttered. With her purse and diaper bag in one hand, and the baby's carrier in the other, she trudged on beneath a sun which had grown hot.

"Pray there's another village around the next curve, Nicky."

"Signor Di Rocche?"

Massimo looked up.

Signor Vercelli's secretary had come into the office where Massimo was going over the latest company audit with the head accountant.

"Forgive the intrusion, but Signor Loti is calling from the Como winery. He wants to talk to you about your relative who was asking about employment this afternoon."

His brows formed a black bar. "What relative?"

"I don't know. He's on line three."

"Thank you."

Massimo picked up the receiver. "Signor Loti?"

The manager explained that a woman named Julie Marchant had asked for a job there. Did Massimo have a particular position in mind for her?

Massimo was absolutely stunned. After telling him Signorina Marchant already had her hands full with his nephew, he thanked him for the call and told him he'd handle this with her himself.

If she thought she could get out of marrying him, she had another think coming.

The accountant's eyes had been watching Massimo during the conversation. When he hung up, the other man said, "No need for explanation. It sounds like you need to take care of things at home. We'll take up where we left off in the morning."

Massimo thanked him, then alerted the pilot he was on his way up to the roof.

Twenty minutes later a forewarned Guido met him outside the villa to explain that Signorina Marchant hadn't arrived home yet.

No woman in Massimo's life had ever tied him up in knots before.

As he started for the estate car parked around the side to

go looking for her, his cell phone rang. He looked at the caller ID. It was the police—

His body broke out in a cold sweat. He clicked on. "This is Signor Di Rocche."

"Signor Di Rocche? Sergeant Santi here. Your company gave me your private number. This is an urgent call, but not grave."

Not grave.

Those last two words pulled him back from the edge of a yawning black void.

Still trying to get his pounding heart to slow down, he asked, "What's the emergency?"

"Two officers found your car abandoned on the main road to Bellagio. While they were checking it out, we received a call from a motorist who saw a woman and a baby walking along the side. He offered her help, but she refused to take it.

"The officers were notified and caught up to her. She says her name is Julie Marchant, and she's the nanny to your nephew. Is that correct?"

His eyes closed tightly. "Yes. Were they hurt in any way?"

"No, *signore*." Thank God. "However the *bambino* is upset."

Massimo could imagine. It had been a hotter day than usual. If she'd run out of formula, and had nothing to eat or drink herself… "Where is she now?"

"With the officers."

"Where are they?"

He gave Massimo the location.

"Tell them to hold her until I get there!"

"*Certamente*. Roadside assistance is on its way to see about your car. They'll be phoning you."

To hell with the damn car. "*Grazie, signore*. I'll be right there."

After assuring Guido everything was under control, he drove toward his destination, uncaring he was going over the speed limit. Once he reached the roadblock and got out of the car, he could see Julie inside the back of the police car with the baby.

Knowing they were safe was all that mattered. The tension started to leave his body.

As he helped her from the police car, imploring blue eyes collided with his searching gaze.

"Massimo—"

Nicky saw him and started crying. He leaned forward as if trying to reach him.

"I…I'm glad you've come. He wants *you*." She handed him the baby.

Nicky snuggled against him. Within seconds he'd calmed down. A lump the size of a golf ball rose in Massimo's throat.

In a few minutes he had them all settled in the estate car and they drove away.

"I don't know what happened to your car," she began. "I saw a red light flash on, then the car just stopped. In case someone crashed into the rear end, I had to get Nicky away from danger. I started walking, but kept as far away from the side of the road as possible."

He fought to get his heart to slow down. "You did the right thing. The point is, how are you?" She looked pale.

"I'm fine, but Nicky's starving. I should have taken more formula with me. I never dreamed we'd be gone this long. Mom was right. I don't know the first thing about being a mother." Her voice trembled.

"Don't beat yourself up. You couldn't have prevented this

from happening no matter how well you planned your outing. You and Nicky weren't harmed. Nothing else matters."

"Yes, it does," she replied in a muffled voice. "I've probably done something terrible to your beautiful new car."

"Forget it."

"How can I when I know you were wrested from work on your first day back at the office."

"Believe it or not, I didn't mind the interruption. The company has more problems than I'd supposed." Hellish problems.

"Which is why you should still be there. I'm sorry for everything, Massimo."

He wished he could crush her in his arms, but that wouldn't be possible until he got her home.

"Did you enjoy your drive before the car stopped on you?" he murmured.

"Y-yes," she stammered.

"Where did you go?"

She averted her eyes. "All over."

"That covers a lot of territory. A simple sightseeing trip?" But he wasn't destined to hear her answer because his cell phone rang. He pulled it from his pocket and clicked on.

When the operator at roadside assistance told him what was wrong with his car, Massimo had a struggle not to laugh out loud. He thanked the man and hung up.

Julie eyed him soulfully. "Was that about the car?"

He nodded. "When I get it back, I'll take you to a service station and teach you which pump is reserved for trucks."

She stared at him with a look of horror on her face. "You mean I put diesel fuel in the tank?"

"Afraid so."

"And that's why it stopped?"

His lips twitched. "It froze the engine."

"Oh no—"

"Fortunately you had the presence of mind to shut off the ignition. No permanent damage was done."

"I hope not." Her voice shook. "All the stations were closed. I finally found a self-service, but it only had one pump," she moaned. "The repair to that engine will be enormous, but I promise I'll repay you every cent."

"That's what insurance is for. In any event a wife doesn't pay her husband back."

He watched her chest heave. "I'm not your wife."

Massimo took a fortifying breath. "Does that mean you don't want to be?"

Her hands formed fists. "I thought you gave me until tonight to make a decision."

He checked his watch. "Technically it will be night in forty-five minutes."

She shook her head. "I'd hoped we could solve this another way. The truth is I went job hunting today without success. On the plane you said you intended for Nicky to explore his American roots. I thought with his Auntie Julie living in the same area, he'd get the chance. But I'm afraid no one will hire me unless I learn Italian.

"The thing is I did something stupid and applied at one of the Di Rocche wineries. You'll probably get a call from them. The poor manager obviously didn't have a job for me. I put him in a terrible position by giving him your name as a reference.

"As soon as we get back to the villa I'll phone him and apologize for taking up his time. I was so determined to find a job today, I didn't stop to think about how I'd put him out. Without knowing your language, I'll never get a job on my own."

His gaze wandered over her features. "Marry me for a year and you'll be fluent without having to pay for lessons."

"Don't make light of this, Massimo," she whispered, sounding tormented.

"It's the only way I know how to survive. When I saw the call from the police, it was like déjà vu."

He saw her throat working. "I…I'm sorry. Honestly."

"Sorry enough to be a mother to Nicky? It's all in your hands."

Her breathing had grown shallow. She was looking everywhere except at him. "Yes. I couldn't leave him now," she confessed.

Satisfied with Julie's response no matter how grudgingly given, Massimo didn't mind that the moment they reached the villa, she hurried into her bedroom as if she were being chased by a tornado.

He fed Nicky and walked him until he fell asleep. After putting him to bed in his crib, he headed for the study to make three important calls. The first was to the priest who would be marrying them.

Once that was accomplished he phoned his uncle. On the fourth ring he heard, "*Pronto*?"

"It's Massimo, Uncle."

"At last! I expected to hear from you before now. How was your first day back at work?"

"It's too soon to ask," he prevaricated. "More to the point, how are you feeling?"

"The doctor says I'm making rapid improvement."

"That's good." Massimo inhaled deeply. "I have other news that can't wait."

"Do I want to hear it?" The wily question held more than a trace of apprehension.

"Let's describe it as bittersweet."

"I like sweets."

"That's why I've arranged for the bank to transfer funds from my account to yours so that you can settle your debt to Signor Ricci, thus freeing Seraphina to pursue her own happiness."

The silence coming from the other end of the phone was a particularly pleasing sound.

Massimo refused to be beholden to any man. He'd borrowed a certain portion of the villa's equity to pay his uncle's debt. The rest he'd invested. It wouldn't take long to recoup a great deal more than the estate was worth.

"Perhaps now the next pill won't be quite so bitter to swallow. I'm marrying Julie next week. Father Bertoldi will be officiating. I hope your doctor will allow you to attend."

Another silence ensued, more eloquent this time.

Massimo knew the doctor had no power over his uncle, who would do what he wanted. It was all a question of his pride.

Could he let it go long enough to witness Massimo's wedding to another Marchant who in recent days had become the Di Rocches' latest nemesis?

To do so would be tantamount to offering posthumous forgiveness to Pietra in front of the family. Massimo wanted to believe there was a part of his uncle that grieved for her. He would have to wait and see.

"Give me another week to work with Signor Vercelli and I'll give you my opinion." Sansone was already having a coronary over Massimo's appearance at the office after a two-year absence. His cousin had reason to be terrified.

"*Dorma bene*, Uncle."

He made the last call to his best friend. "*Ciao*, Cesar."

"I was just thinking about you. How's it going with your nephew?"

"I'm crazy about him."

"And his *bellissima* aunt?"

"That's why I'm phoning. I didn't want you to hear this from anyone else."

"What is it?"

"I'm getting married."

Cesar let out a cry of disbelief. "So now I'm going to be alone!"

"With all those female fans wild about you, I'm not worried."

He chuckled. "I knew this day would have to come sometime, but who would have expected another Di Rocche would fall prey to another Marchant—

"Congratulations, Massimo. Tell me when and where, and I'll be there to celebrate with you."

"You don't know what that means."

"I think I do."

"One day your number will be up, too." Massimo wanted to believe his own words because there'd been a woman in Cesar's past named Sarah who'd hurt him in a way that had caused his cousin to close off his heart ever since.

"You think?" Cesar's laugh rang hollow.

"I *know*," Massimo declared. "Drive safely. I want you here in one piece."

Julie followed her mother out of the bridal boutique into the midafternoon sun. With the wedding scheduled for the day after tomorrow, she was relieved to have found a dress that didn't need to be altered. The manager assured her everything would be delivered to the villa tomorrow.

"What a shame you can't be married here in Bellagio. The whole place is a garden."

"Mom—slow down a minute."

Her mother eyed her curiously. "What's wrong? Ever since I got here you've been unusually quiet, even around my grandson, who's positively thriving, by the way."

Julie was glad her mother had noticed, but she had something else on her mind.

"You *do* understand the reason for this marriage."

"Of course. You can't stay in a single man's house while you're here, not even for the baby's sake."

"It's only temporary. A year, possibly less. So you can see why I'm going through with it?"

"I'm aware how much you love Nicky, otherwise you wouldn't have approached Massimo before your father and I met him."

A small cry of surprise escaped. "How did you know that?"

"I know my daughter a lot better than you give me credit for. I thought it strange you'd gone out just before he arrived at the town house. Once he presented himself, everything went too smoothly. You didn't bat an eyelash about working for him.

"Now that I'm here, it's clear to both your father and me you've fallen for Nicky's uncle. Don't bother to deny it. It doesn't suit you to lie. You were born with a headstrong resistant streak worse than your brother's. Between the two of you I went gray early. But I have to say in this instance, I approve."

This had to be a first for her mother.

"I'm not blind, Julie. He looks like Adonis come to life. But putting that aside for the moment, I'd say you've met your match. What I wonder is if you realize he's not going to let you get away with anything. He's not like your father."

"Let's not bring Dad into this discussion."

"Because he's perfect and I'm not?"

She moaned. "I didn't say that."

"No. *I'm* the one who brought it up. Let's agree the truth lies somewhere in between. The point being that there will be times when Massimo won't be malleable like your dad. Too many times of letting your pride get in the way of common sense and you may lose him the way I lost your father."

Julie was dumbstruck by the admission.

"Massimo's not mine to lose, Mom. We hardly know each other."

"Yet he's willing to take you on because he knows it's best for Nicky. That tells me more about my soon-to-be son-in-law than you can imagine. I'd say you've got a lot of work to do."

"It wouldn't matter. There are things he didn't tell you. He was scarred growing up."

"Who hasn't been at one time or other? Though I'm happy with Lem, I'd give anything to do certain things over again, but those opportunities have passed. Not so for you."

She studied her mother for a minute. "You seem different."

Her parent looked sheepish. "Since Lem and I went back to Honolulu, I've been seeing a therapist."

"You?"

"I know. I should have done it years ago. It took losing Shawn…"

"Oh, Mom—" Forgetting they were walking along the colorful street in plain view of locals and tourists, Julie hugged her. "I'm glad you're here."

"Do you know that's the first time I can remember you saying that to me in ages?" Her mother sniffed. "I didn't tell you that to make you feel bad, so don't jump down my throat."

"I won't." Julie squeezed her eyes tightly, realizing not everything had been her mother's fault. They weren't mother and daughter for nothing. Julie had been a difficult child, and still was.

The day after tomorrow she'd be Massimo's difficult bride. That's what her mother was trying to tell her. On the walk home from town, her parent also managed to impress upon her the sanctity of her vows.

Although she and Massimo had an understanding about what would and *wouldn't* go on in their marriage, she couldn't ignore the fact that things were going to change.

Somehow knowing he was going to be her husband made her more nervous than usual.

By the time they reached the villa, she excused herself to freshen up before facing him. But she needn't have worried. According to Gina, he hadn't returned from Milan yet.

Her father had taken Nicky out in the garden for a stroll and, intent on spending the evening with her parents, she left the nursery and started downstairs. Midway she paused because she thought she heard a familiar voice filtering up from the foyer.

No…it couldn't be.

Another few steps and she saw that the housekeeper had opened the door. Brent stood in the entrance. His sober gaze flew to hers. "Hello, Julie."

CHAPTER NINE

JULIE would never have imagined him coming here.

"It's good to see you." His voice sounded thick.

Had he come to try to stop her from getting married? Her father must have told him about her plans. She hadn't thought Brent knew anything.

His short-cropped sandy hair was so familiar she felt a pang for the memories the sight of him conjured. But that was all. Julie couldn't honestly tell him the same thing back. Not anymore.

He stared at her out of pain-filled hazel eyes. Until now she hadn't realized how all-American he looked. It took the setting of this ornate Italian villa to make him stand out in his corporate white shirt and blue suit.

"Whether I'm welcome or not, I had to come. We need to talk, but I don't want to do it here. Will you take a drive with me?"

Lia refrained from saying what was on her mind, but her eyes spoke volumes. Massimo would be home soon, and he wouldn't expect Brent to be here. He might think she'd encouraged him to come.

The disturbing thought of Massimo walking in on them prompted her next decision.

"Let me get my purse and I'll be right down."

He looked relieved, probably because he'd expected a refusal. "I'll wait for you in my rental car."

She nodded before turning to Lia. "My father's taking care of Nicky right now. Tell my parents I'll be back in a few minutes."

Julie rushed up to her bedroom, unable to credit he'd flown all this way. Brent didn't part with his money easily. He would have been forced to dip into his savings for an airline ticket. For him to do that made a statement she couldn't ignore.

Somehow she managed to slip out of the villa without her parents seeing her. Not that it would have mattered. They wouldn't have interfered. Quite the opposite where her mother was concerned. Julie was just glad she didn't have to explain herself. The time for that would come later.

When she walked out to the courtyard, he moved to open the door for her. She would have climbed in, but he put his arms around her and pulled her close. He was trembling.

"I've been such a fool, Julie." She sensed he was going to kiss her.

"Please don't."

She pulled away from him. Though she'd been in his arms many times before, she'd never known him to be this emotional. She realized he'd come here with no other agenda than to be with her. A part of her was flattered that he hadn't given up on her so easily, but as she'd told him before she left Sonoma, they would never have made it.

Still, he'd flown all this way. She could give him a few more minutes, but in the distance she could hear the whir of rotor blades coming closer. She didn't want Massimo to see them.

"There's a villa open to the public two miles from here. We can talk in the parking lot."

Once she was seated, he went around to the driver's side and started the car. She gave him directions and they took off. When they came upon the villa in question, he drove in and parked next to the other cars.

"Julie—" He turned to her with tears in his eyes. "When you didn't return my phone calls, I phoned your father but couldn't reach him. After that I tried your mother to find out the address of the villa so I could come and see you.

"That's when your stepfather informed me she'd left for Italy to attend your wedding."

So *that's* how he'd known where to come.

Brent shook his head. "It blew me away."

She was blown away, too. Nothing seemed quite real yet.

"I know you're only doing it for Nicky's sake, but you don't love Nicky's uncle. You couldn't!"

That's where Brent was wrong.

"If I hadn't made the biggest mistake of my life by not coming to the funeral, you and I would be getting married. Do you hear what I'm saying, Julie? Call it off and marry me. I love you. I'll help you raise Nicky."

The right words said by the wrong man.

He grasped her hand. "When you told me you wanted to be a mother to him, I got angry that you would put him before us. It felt like all my dreams for a future with you were smashed."

"I know. It was the blackest moment of my life."

"I was a jerk, only thinking of myself, but I've changed. It's not too late for us."

"I'm afraid it is."

"Give me one good reason why."

In a few words she explained about Shawn and Pietra's will. "So you see, I have to stay in Bellagio if I want to help take care of the baby. For both of us to be unmarried doesn't look right."

"Then I'll get a software job in Milan and move here. We could be married and you could tend Nicky every day. I'll be his other uncle."

"No, Brent."

"You're like a stone wall. I can't get through to you. I've missed you! It's been weeks since we were together. Say you've missed me, too."

A moan escaped her throat. Once upon a time she'd loved him in her own way, but it seemed so long ago, even though it had been less than a month.

The truth was she felt no accompanying rush of joy at seeing him again. To marry him she would have to feel a desire for him so great, she couldn't imagine being separated from him.

She would have to feel the way she felt around Massimo every second of the day and night.

When she thought about how quickly Nicky's uncle had supplanted thoughts of any other man in her mind, she was frightened by his power over her emotions.

"You've changed," he muttered.

"I'm afraid Shawn's and Pietra's deaths changed me."

"Of course, but I'm talking about you, the woman I fell for. There's a difference in you." He let out a deep breath. "You feel something for this man, don't you?"

How to describe Massimo. It wasn't possible.

"He's a remarkable human being."

"Oh, I think he means a lot more to you than that."

Brent was beginning to sound defensive. More like the old Brent. In fairness to him she understood that no one liked to be turned down. It hurt.

"I'm sorry, Brent."

"So am I."

She looked around. "I've been gone too long. Please take me back to the villa."

"Before your fiancé comes looking for you?" he asked aggressively.

"I wasn't going to say that."

"You didn't have to. He's been the ghost between us since I saw you in the hallway of the villa."

On that half-broken, half-bitter note he started the car.

Massimo had just lived through the day from hell. If he hadn't known he'd be coming home to Nicky and Julie, he couldn't bear to think about the status of his life. It made him sick deep in his gut.

After a shower and shave, he pulled on trousers and a sport shirt before going in search of Julie. With her parents housed in the villa, they could spend all the time they wanted with Nicky. This suited Massimo, who had plans to take their daughter out alone for the evening.

As well as certain things he needed to finalize with her before the wedding ceremony, he had to talk to her about something critically important to their future.

Lia met him on the stair landing. "I was just coming to find you."

She'd been with his family so many years, he knew when something was bothering her. "Is Nicky all right?"

"Yes. He's with his grandfather."

"Then what's wrong?"

"It's about Signorina Marchant."

What now? "Go on."

"She isn't here."

He didn't like the sound of that. "Where is she?"

"Signor Walton came to the villa earlier. She left with him in his car."

Massimo reeled. Her ex had actually come here?

"Do you know if she'd been expecting him?"

His housekeeper lifted her hands. "I can't say, but Signorina Marchant seemed surprised."

And happy?

He decided not to ask Lia that question. He might not like the answer.

"Do you have any idea where they went?

"No."

He could see his plans for the evening evaporating. Several black thoughts entered his mind. It appeared she'd decided to return her ex's calls after all. To fly all this way meant he was hoping to prevent their marriage from taking place.

Massimo rubbed the front of his chest abstractedly. Depending on how persuasive Signor Walton could be, it might be hours before her return. He didn't want to entertain images of her being with the man she'd once planned to marry.

Even if Lia was right and his arrival had come as a surprise to Julie, she'd been receptive enough to drive off with him. A man didn't go out of his way to this extent unless he wanted her back, and she knew it! Subconsciously she'd probably been waiting and hoping for this moment.

When Massimo recalled Seraphina's welcome at the airport, he wouldn't put anything past Julie's ex.

He couldn't help but wonder how long the two of them had been intimate. Evidently, long enough that he wasn't about to give her up without a struggle.

Massimo ground his teeth, realizing he had no claim on her yet.

What did he mean "yet"?

She might have agreed to marry Massimo, but she'd made it clear nothing was going to change in their personal relationship. She planned to remain a free agent after they'd become man and wife.

Julie had drawn conclusions about their marriage of convenience. They would both pursue their own desires as long as they were discreet.

He'd agreed to the terms in order to get her to say yes to him, but he'd known deep down that when it came to the crunch, he couldn't live by them. Signor Walton's appearance on Massimo's territory was proof of that.

Restless as a caged panther, he went to the kitchen for a cup of coffee. Preferably black enough for a spoon to stand in. What he really needed was something much stronger of course. But he had to remember there were guests in the house. And there was Nicky, who deserved the best Massimo had to give him.

After swallowing the last dregs of the hot liquid, he realized he couldn't stay in here fuming indefinitely. Knowing the baby would always give him a satisfying welcome, he headed for the veranda.

This time of year it was the most pleasant spot to be. Julie's parents preferred to be outside. Without doubt it looked out on the view he loved most.

Nearing the end of the hallway, he saw movement out of the corner of his eye. His heart missed a beat to see Julie let herself in the front door. Apparently she was alone for the moment.

Her composure didn't tell him anything. He moved closer. No sign of tears on that peaches-and-cream complexion.

"Good evening."

He heard her take a surprised breath. "I…I didn't realize you were standing there."

And wished he weren't?

That was too bad because she was going to have to get used to his presence on a permanent basis.

"I understand your ex-boyfriend came to Bellagio."

"Yes." She smoothed some blond strands of hair behind her shell-like ear. "His visit was totally unexpected."

He believed her. One thing he knew about Julie. She didn't have a dishonest bone in her body.

Normally she wore lipstick. If she'd left wearing some, it was gone now. The thought of her being kissed senseless by the other man made Massimo feel he had been kicked in the gut. Had she responded to her former lover with equal hunger?

The memory of her mouth opening to the pressure of Massimo's kiss still sent a heat wave through every part of him.

"Why didn't you invite him in?"

A subtle blush broke out on her skin. Telling evidence she and Signor Walton had exchanged more than conversation. Had he taken her to a hotel where they'd been able to make love? She'd been gone long enough!

Massimo would love to know if she'd left the house wearing her usual ponytail. He noticed it was free flowing at the moment. In fact it looked slightly disheveled in an enticing way. He groaned to think of the other man's fingers twisted in all that gold silk.

"Brent didn't want to intrude."

No. He just wanted her back.

"This is going to be your home, Julie. You have every right to conduct your life the way you want."

He'd given her the opening if she was ready to tell him she couldn't marry him after all. Not that he would let her out of her commitment to him, but he could pretend to be a civilized man.

"Thank you."

The politeness had to stop. "Is he still outside?"

Her blue eyes darkened perceptibly. "No."

"Are you expecting him later?"

"No. He's gone."

She'd said the magic word. Still, he wanted total verification. "Until tomorrow?"

She looked away. "Brent didn't know you'd been named Nicky's guardian. Now that he undertands the baby has to remain here, he's out of my life for good."

The last had been said so quietly, Massimo sensed she was torn by the choice she'd had to make out of love for her brother's child. But for her commitment to her little nephew...

"Has Nicky been put down yet?" she asked.

"No. It's warmer than usual tonight. Lia says your father's been outside with him. That leaves us free to spend some much-needed time together. Let's go."

Her gaze swerved to his in alarm. A real dampener if he let it get to him, but his desire to be alone with her prevailed.

"Where?"

"For a ride. There are things we need to discuss."

He noticed a tiny pulse start to throb at the base of her throat. "Your car's not back from the shop yet."

"We'll be taking the estate car."

She fiddled with the hem of the pale blue lace-edged top covering her womanly hips. "Maybe we shouldn't leave the baby."

One dark brow dipped. "Do you hear him crying?"

"No."

"Then let's not stay to fix something that isn't broken."

Without giving her time to reconsider, he ushered her outside the villa and around the side where Guido kept the other car parked. After admiring her shapely legs while he helped her get in, he retraced the route he'd followed to the private dock the week before.

"I didn't realize you were taking us out on the boat." Those were the first words she'd spoken since leaving the house. From the sound of it, she greeted the idea with reluctance.

"Night is one of the best times to see the lake. The temperature's perfect right now."

"The baby's going to miss us, Massimo."

"I'm sure of it, but you and I need a break. We've been caring for him nonstop for close to a month. Yesterday your mother indicated she wanted an evening to herself with Nicky. I thought we'd give it to her. Your father's there to help."

On that note he levered himself from the car. He would have gone round for Julie, but she moved too fast for him. She'd been giving off signals she wanted to be left alone. Massimo decided to accommodate her, and let her reach the boat before he did.

While he untied the ropes, she had to lift her skirt far enough to step down inside. He cast her a sideways glance, enjoying the view of feminine limbs on display.

His gaze followed her to a seat in the back. When he realized it was the farthest distance from the helm, a half smile broke the corner of his mouth. Since the bedroom was below deck, she'd chosen the safest place on the craft to avoid him.

Pushing the boat away from the pier, he jumped on board. "There's a life preserver in the seat locker next to you. Humor me and put it on."

She did his bidding. Ten minutes into their night cruise she joined him up front. They were almost to the island.

"The lakeshore looks like clusters of diamonds linked by diamond chains." Her eyes shifted to his. "It's a sight everyone should be able to see at least once in their life."

The sight of her pure profile with the hair blowing away from her face made his breath catch. "That sounds almost mournful."

"I was thinking of Pietra. When she married Shawn, she had no idea she wouldn't b—" The rest didn't come out. Only a quiet sob.

After a minute, "I'm sorry."

He grimaced. "For what? In the odd moment I get choked up, too."

She wiped her eyes. "How was work today?"

That was the kind of question a wife asked her husband after a day's separation. In Julie's case he assumed she was deliberately steering the conversation in a direction that had no connection to the man who'd flown to see her today.

"Do you really want to know?"

Her gaze met his head-on. "Do you think I don't?" she snapped. "Whatever affects you will inevitably affect me and Nicky. I hate secrets. After what Vigo put me through, I never want to be in the dark again."

Massimo cut the motor and dropped anchor. Now that activity on the lake had subsided, the island was virtually deserted. He turned in the seat to face her.

"The situation at Di Rocche's is worse than I thought." Her brows formed a delicate frown. "About three years ago the company slowly began to lose money. I was vice president over acquisition of assets at the time. I knew the business was growing at a comfortable rate. The problem had to be elsewhere.

"Without anyone's knowledge I started looking into the accounts. Certain discrepancies showed a particular pattern leading to the expenditures department, Sansone's domain.

"I had my suspicions as to why. In time I felt he was the

person responsible, but I needed proof. The only way to obtain the information I needed was to have him investigated."

"That *is* serious," she murmured.

Massimo nodded. "My cousin's antipathy for me is well-known, but I didn't think he'd go so far as to rob his own father's company. I don't know if it was prompted by pure greed or revenge."

She cocked her head. "Why revenge?"

"To get back at my uncle for making me a vice president instead of him."

"He's sick."

Julie didn't know the half of it. "Relations within the family were already explosive. I knew that if I went to my uncle with what I'd discovered, further investigation might show my other cousins were involved. Then everything really would blow apart because too much blood had already been spilled."

"You think they're guilty, too?"

"I'm not sure. To be honest, I didn't want to know. I decided I would leave Italy for good and let my uncle eventually come to his own conclusions without my playing a part in the denouement.

"I knew it was a risk to leave. When the time came for heads to roll, Sansone would already have planted seeds of blame in my direction.

"Sure enough Pietra's will changed history. I've returned under heavy suspicion at the company. My uncle's been forced to downsize. Loyal employees have lost their jobs. Sansone has done what he could to make me the scapegoat for their anger."

"That's preposterous! Your uncle welcomed you like a conquering hero."

Though her emotions might still be caught up in her feelings for the man who'd just held her in his arms, her defense of Massimo was something to cherish.

"Uncle Aldo's an intelligent man and probably knows why I left, but he's too hurt and too proud to admit his children are the ones at fault. He's determined to make me CEO in the hope I'll employ controls over Sansone. Supposedly that will frustrate his ability to do more damage in future without exposing him."

A shadow fell across her face. "That's going to entail enormous responsibility."

Her comment led him to believe she didn't like the idea of him putting in those kinds of hours away from Nicky. When it came to his priorities, Massimo was way ahead of her in that regard.

"Sansone will never stand for it, so it's a moot point."

"What would he do if you were voted in to fill the top position?"

"I don't have an answer for that."

"Well, I don't think you should stay around here to find out."

Adrenaline filled his bloodstream. "Explain what you mean."

"Did you ever tell Pietra your suspicions?"

"No. I didn't want her to know anything."

"Then I think you should forget putting Nicky in touch with his Italian side. She wouldn't hold you to it if she had any idea what you've uncovered. Admit that your desire to honor her wishes is the only reason you brought Nicky back here."

Her instincts were uncanny. He raised his head. "That's a big part of it."

"Was Seraphina the rest? Did she ever indicate a desire to go to Central America with you, or join you there?"

He stared into her eyes. "Yes, but I knew she wouldn't last a day. She's what you Americans call high maintenance."

Massimo could hear her mind working. "Then you should leave this seething cauldron and take Nicky away until he becomes a man. At that point tell him the truth and let him decide what he wants to do about his money and his heritage."

Massimo pursed his lips. "That's a very tempting thought. Are you suggesting we go back to Sonoma? Your father's still waiting to find the right renter."

"No. You're an archaeologist with work to do. You need to go back to Cancuen as soon as possible. Lia's told me you're constantly besieged by phone calls from your colleagues needing your input."

Julie and his housekeeper had gotten close in the short time she had been here. That was a rare occurrence. Lia didn't confide in most people.

"In case you've forgotten, I've acquired a nephew."

"Don't any of them have children?"

"A few."

"Do they live on the site, too?"

"One couple does."

"Then?"

He studied her through veiled eyes. "You actually meant it when you told me you'd live with me and Nicky in the jungle."

"Yes, I did."

Incredible.

"Do you still mean it?"

She nodded. "I can't see that staying here could ever make you or Nicky happy. If it's possible, every person should be able to do what they were meant to do."

Unable to restrain himself, he grasped her forearms and pulled her to him so she stood in between his legs. "What do you think you were meant to do?" He could feel the tremors that shook her body.

"If you'd asked me before the accident, I couldn't have told you. But now…my future seems bound with Nicky's. Perhaps I'll stumble on to my life's work in the process."

He brushed his lips against hers. "Maybe we'll turn you into an archaeologist."

"Maybe. What's it like in Cancuen?"

"Let's go below where it's more comfortable and I'll tell you."

"I'd prefer to stay up here."

His hands cradled the sides of her neck. "All I want to do is hold you for a little while. Do you have any idea how beautiful you are?"

"Don't say those things to me, Massimo."

"Why? You admitted I'm a red-blooded male."

"That's not the point. We have an understanding."

"Yes. We do. We agreed to follow our own desires as long as we were discreet. Being alone on the Isola Comacina fulfills that requirement."

Sensing her breathing had become more erratic, he drew her face closer. "The other night we comforted each other. Tonight is different. I want to kiss you because I need to kiss you or go a little mad."

"You're missing the girlfriend you left in Guatemala," she argued. "If you're really serious about going back to the jungle, then surely you can wait a little longer."

"That's where you're wrong," he whispered huskily before covering her mouth with his own.

A sound like an aching moan came from her throat, igniting the passion he'd been trying unsuccessfully to suppress.

"You taste divine, do you know that?" His hunger for her

had already flared out of control. He found himself devouring her mouth. Her skin, her hair, everything about her had intoxicated him.

She might have been with her former lover earlier in the evening, but her response right now exhibited a hunger that proved her feelings for the other man posed little threat to Massimo.

That was all he needed to know before lifting her in his arms. The feel of her curving warmth against his body had set him on fire. By the time they reached the dimly lit bedroom below deck, his whole frame was trembling with needs she'd aroused without knowing it.

He followed her down on the bed, burying his face in her neck. "I want you, Julie." He threaded his fingers through her golden silk. "You have no idea how much." His mouth plundered hers again. "I want to make love to you all night."

He rolled on his back taking her with him. Slowly he moved his hands over her waist and hips, loving her shape. Her body gave a voluptuous shiver.

"Was that your answer?" he asked as his lips grazed every inch of her face and throat.

"First let me ask you a question," came her tremulous voice.

He pressed a kiss to the side of her enticing mouth. "What is it?"

"Have you made up your mind to leave Italy?"

His hands stilled on the soft arms he'd been caressing. It was no idle question. "Why?"

"Because if you have, there's no reason for us to get married."

"The wedding's off."

Two heads swerved in Julie's direction as she walked into

the nursery. Her parents were standing on either side of the crib. Before her interruption they'd been talking quietly. Her darling Nicky lay sound asleep.

"I guess we don't have to ask how your evening went," her father said.

Her mother's brows lifted. "Not because of Brent surely."

Julie came to a standstill. "You knew he'd been at the villa earlier?"

They both nodded.

"This has nothing to do with him."

She knew what her mom wanted to say, that this new development was Julie's fault. But by some miracle her mother held her tongue. The therapy really was working.

"Where's Massimo?" she asked.

"Putting the car away." For once it was her father who gave her the odd stare, making her uncomfortable.

"You might as well know the truth, Dad. The only reason marriage came up in the first place was to silence the family gossip about us living together at the villa. But Massimo has decided he doesn't want to stay in Italy. There are too many problems I won't go into right now. Needless to say, his heart isn't here.

"We talked about it on the boat tonight. As soon as he informs his uncle there isn't going to be a wedding after all, he's planning to take Nicky back to Guatemala. I'll be going with them."

Still her father said nothing, increasing her nervousness.

"While we live there, no one will care about our relationship. It won't matter if anyone judges us. We can carry on raising Nicky together without having to be locked in a marriage neither of us would have chosen. This way we'll both get what we want."

An aura of sadness seemed to have enveloped her dad. "Be careful over what you want, honey," he muttered. "Sometimes you get it."

Was he talking about himself or her? A chill ran through her body. She didn't know her father like this.

"The jungle isn't for everyone," he reminded her.

Julie wasn't used to her dad doing all the talking.

"Massimo said the same thing. Tomorrow afternoon he's taking me and the baby to the doctor to start all our immunizations. We're going to give it a trial run.

"If I can't handle it, or we feel it isn't good for Nicky, then we'll move to Mexico and he'll buy a house in San Cristobal. He says it's a charming colonial town in the north, twenty minutes by helicopter from the Mayan ruins at Palenque.

"He has friends who oversee a dig site there. They've begged him to come for a long time. Some of the married archaeologists who have children live in the town. He says they love it.

"But whatever happens, we'll be much closer to both of you. Massimo has promised to fly us to Hawaii and California once a month for weekend visits so Nicky can be with you.

"He keeps a large apartment in Mexico City and goes there quite often. You can fly down and stay with us."

She bit her lip. "I hope you aren't too disappointed."

Her father looked puzzled. "Over what?"

"You know. About me not getting married. You flew all this way for it."

"At some point I would have come to see you and our grandson anyway. What you do or don't do with your life is your business. You're a grown woman. I can tell Nicky is crazy about you. That's the important thing."

"He adores Massimo."

Her father smiled. "So we noticed."

"Do you know motherhood becomes you?" This from her mom who only a month ago told her she'd be hopeless in that department.

"I...I'm only his aunt, but I love him to death."

"It shows," they said in unison.

For the first time in her life Julie felt tongue-tied around her parents. "If you're going to stay in here a while longer, I'm going to bed. It's been a long day.

"Maybe tomorrow morning we can walk to town with Nicky and have breakfast together. I'll take the wedding dress back at the same time."

"Sounds good, honey."

"Well, good night, then." She kissed her dad, then her mom.

"Don't worry about Nicky, darling. I'll stay in here with him tonight. Sleep well."

Sleep well?

That was a joke.

Long after she'd brushed her teeth and climbed into bed, she lay there wide-awake. Her mind kept going over what had happened on the boat.

Once she'd told Massimo that if they weren't going to stay in Bellagio, there was no point in getting married, the tension in the bedroom had become thick. You'd have thought a dark cloud had descended on them.

With the advantage of surprise on her side, she'd eased herself off his rock-hard body and had darted out of the room to the top deck.

To leave him when she'd been on the brink of rapture was the hardest thing she'd ever had to do. In fact she didn't know how she'd found the physical strength to deny herself.

But the mind had more power over the body than she'd realized. Julie hadn't been able to forget what he'd told her about his mother, who wanted to be loved for herself and no other reason.

If anyone understood her motives for refusing to marry his father, Julie did.

Obviously Massimo's father *did* love her. He ended up proving it by living with her. He gave her two children. But she didn't know his true feelings at the time.

No woman wanted to go through with a wedding ceremony orchestrated by an outside agenda, or with anyone other than the man who loved her.

She crushed a portion of the sheet in her fist. No woman wanted to be used to fill a man's needs because she was available.

Julie had needs. They'd almost overpowered her tonight when Massimo had started to make love to her. It would have been so easy to succumb. It would have been heaven. She knew that.

Shawn and Pietra hadn't held back, but in their case everything was different because they were two people who had met and fallen in love. They experienced the joy of knowing they were equals in a pure love. It was only natural they wanted that love blessed by marriage.

Out of that thrilling union, Nicky was born.

Tears trickled beneath her closed lids, wetting her lashes. Julie wasn't Nicky's first choice for a mother. As for Massimo, he was a bachelor who'd never been in the market for a wife.

Some prize she was.

A woman torn in a war between her love for her nephew

and his uncle, and absolutely unable to walk away from either of them.

She buried her face in the pillow to stifle the sobs that shook her body.

CHAPTER TEN

A WEEK later Massimo drove everyone to the airport in Milan to see her parents off. Much as she loved them, it was a relief to be alone again. Since the wedding had been canceled, the atmosphere in the villa had changed.

No one talked about it. Not the staff. Not Massimo, who went to work every day and played the perfect host every evening. Not Julie's parents, who continued to enjoy Nicky and take care of him.

They didn't argue. Life was pleasant and went along as if there'd never been any plans for a wedding. It had all been so unnatural Julie wanted to scream.

"Where are we going?" Julie had assumed they would be driving straight back to the villa. She looked over her shoulder. All was quiet in the backseat, but she couldn't tell if Nicky was asleep or not.

Massimo flicked her a glance she couldn't read. "We'll be leaving for Guatemala when you and Nicky have finished your immunization treatments. That gives us three weeks to prepare. You'll need the proper clothes, so we'll start with that first."

For a man who couldn't wait to get back to the jungle, he didn't show the excitement she would have expected. He said and did all the right things, but everything seemed different now.

Since the incident on the boat when she'd brought a halt to their lovemaking, he hadn't tried to be physical with her again. Even the camaraderie she'd always felt between them seemed to have vanished.

When she truly thought about it, he'd started treating her like a real nanny.

He'd never made her feel that way until now. Their biological connection to Nicky had put their relationship on a different level. Or so she'd thought… But this was what she'd wanted all along, so it made no sense that she cared, which was a lie because she was madly in love with him.

"Your car seems to be working beautifully. I'm so relieved no permanent damage was done."

"I told you it wasn't serious."

She couldn't stand the emotional distance between them.

"You haven't told me anything about your family lately. What did your uncle say?"

"About what?" he muttered, sounding impatient.

"Our change in wedding plans."

She saw his hands grip the wheel a little tighter. "There's only one thing on his mind."

Julie took a deep breath. "He wants you to be the one in full charge of his company."

"That's right. Make no mistake. It's in trouble. There's one capable man in his employ who could pull it out, but he's not family, and it would mean my cousin's head. Uncle Aldo's still not willing to do that."

She shifted in the seat. "Every day that you're still in Italy, he's probably hoping you'll change your mind."

"He's counting on it."

The tension with Sansone had to be unbearable.

Julie gave him a surreptitious glance. She'd been toying with an idea, but needed to know all the facts first. "How's his heart?"

"The doctor says he'll be fine if he sticks to his regimen."

Hearing that, her adrenaline kicked in. "In that case, let's all leave now."

He shook his dark head. "You know that's impossible."

Massimo only said that because he was no longer a free agent. Through a tragic stroke of fate, the three of them were stuck together. He was responsible for his nephew, whose needs had to come first.

Out of the necessity to be with Nicky because she loved him, Julie had forced Massimo to hire her. She'd become his excess baggage, not his wife.

"You go to Guatemala now and get things ready for us," she urged. "Nicky and I will fly to Hawaii. Mother wants us to come whenever we can. With Lem busy on his court case, she'll be thrilled for the company.

"We'll stay with her and finish up our immunizations. If you give me a list of things to buy, I'll do it there. I'd rather.

"Please, Massimo—let's go back to the villa and start packing before your uncle comes up with some new reason to keep you here," she begged. "We'll fly commerical so he won't know we've left until after we're gone."

He continued to maneuver the car with his usual expertise through the heavy traffic. At first she thought he'd ignored her plea, but minutes later she realized they'd made a circle and had come out on the main road leading to Bellagio.

Massimo *wanted* to leave immediately.

She'd known it, felt it in her heart. That would account for his brooding behavior over the last few days. Maybe no one else noticed it, but she did. They'd been together long enough for her to read his moods.

Certainly Pietra had understood her brother. She'd been able to see he was only really alive when he did what made him happy. That's why she'd urged him to go to Guatemala in the first place.

When they came to a stop in the courtyard, he unexpectedly undid his seat belt and leaned across the gearshift to press a hard, swift kiss to her mouth.

"I feel like I've been let out of prison and have you to thank for it. After I take Nicky inside, I'll phone the airlines. Over lunch we'll make a list of things to do and get started packing."

A new chapter in her life was about to begin. She was going to the jungle, a place she'd only heard about or seen in films. Knowing she'd be living with Massimo in a hut beneath the green canopy he'd told her so much about caused the fire inside her to burn white hot.

Throughout the next twenty-four hours, the feel of his compelling mouth stayed with her, keeping that ache for him acute. She could hardly concentrate on anything that needed doing before they left.

But she needn't have worried. Massimo could do the work of ten men. By noon of the next day they were on their way to Atlanta where they would board different flights to their destinations.

Guido drove them to the airport. A tearful Lia had waved them off. Julie had hugged her hard, thanking her for everything.

Massimo kissed the housekeeper on both cheeks, promising they'd be back. But Julie knew that wouldn't happen until Sansone had been caught, and a new CEO installed.

It went without saying that Massimo would be back if

anything happened to his uncle. Julie could only hope he'd stay well for a long time. Years. That way Massimo wouldn't be burdened with another weight of guilt for something he couldn't help. There'd been too much pain in his life. He didn't need more.

Julie's flight to Hawaii left before his. Massimo managed to obtain permission to board the first-class compartment with her. He helped her with Nicky.

When she saw the way his eyes closed tightly while he hugged the baby goodbye, she realized he loved his nephew as if he were a son of his own flesh. She understood.

At some point over the past month the lines had been blurred. She felt like Nicky's mother. Massimo had said she needed Nicky. He'd been right. The truth was, she wanted to be his legal mother so she could call him her little boy in every sense of the word.

Tears flooded her eyes because the gorgeous black-haired male holding her adorable boy had become her whole world. To have to wait three weeks until she saw Massimo again didn't bear thinking about.

He settled the baby carrier in the seat harness, then turned to Julie, who'd strapped herself in the next seat. His fiery black eyes swept over her features with an anxious look she'd never observed before.

"I'll call you every night. You have my cell phone. Call me day or night. If there's no service, you have the number of the established phone line at the compound. They'll contact me immediately if anything's wrong."

"There won't be." She smiled, trying to hide her chaotic emotions. "We're going to be fine. My mother will see to that. She's not going to believe it when I phone her and let her know I'm in Hawaii with her little grandson."

A tiny pulse throbbed at the corner of his mouth, evidence this parting from Nicky was an emotional one for him, too.

"Stop being so damn brave, Julie. You think I don't realize you've got the brunt of the work and the worry?" His breathing sounded ragged. "Let's hope the rest of the immunizations don't make either of you feel any sicker."

"We'll live. Luckily he's a big strong boy just like his uncle. Now you've got to get off this plane: The flight attendant's been throwing signals your way."

His jaw hardened. "I have half a mind to fly to Hawaii with you. Getting away from Italy was the main thing."

"No, Massimo. I'm going to feel a lot better knowing you've prepared everything for us ahead of time. When you explained about the way we have to live at the site, I was overwhelmed with all you have to do to make a home for us."

She saw his gaze fly to the baby. "After three weeks Nicky won't even know me."

"Want to bet? His whole world lights up whenever you come in the room. Last night his eyes followed every move you made. It's so touching to watch."

That brought his attention back to her. "I'll meet your plane in Guatemala City. We'll take another flight from there to the Petén."

"It will be a brand-new experience."

His expression grim, he leaned down. "Miss me a little," he whispered thickly before pressing another kiss to her mouth. This time he drank deeply, almost as if he were trying to draw her soul from her body.

Unable to help herself, she found herself kissing him back with a fervor that would make her blush when she recalled it later. By then it would be too late to berate herself for her weakness.

When he finally relinquished her lips she cried softly, "Be safe."

"Julie—"

"They're closing the doors, sir," the flight attendant said, preventing Julie from hearing the rest.

Their eyes met one more time. Her gaze clung to him before his tall fit body strode down the aisle. As he disappeared from the cabin, taking her heart with him, she could hear the warning her father had given her after she'd called off the wedding.

Be careful over what you want, honey. Sometimes you get it.

"Oh, Nicky…" She groaned. Massimo wouldn't have kissed her like that if he didn't care a little. "I've made the biggest mistake of my life. Now it's too late."

Travelers flock to Guatemala because it offers Central America in concentrated form; its volcanoes are the highest and most active, its Mayan ruins the most impressive, its earthquakes the most devastating and its history decidedly intense.

Julie had shivered with excitement after reading the statement on the small brochure provided by the airline. Only the knowledge that Massimo was waiting for her as soon as she cleared customs took away any accompanying apprehension or fatigue after the second leg of her flight from Los Angeles.

Three weeks apart from him had felt like a year. If it hadn't been for his nightly phone calls that assured her he was all right, she wouldn't have made it. Though Nicky was the focus of their conversation, she'd managed to get an idea of what his days were like.

The customs official welcomed her, then handed back her

passport. Julie thanked him. Her body trembled with growing excitement as she put it back in her purse.

"Come on, Nicky. Let's go find your uncle." She picked up his baby carrier. They passed through the doors leading to the lounge area.

But one look around and she discovered Massimo wasn't here!

Her disappointment at not seeing him right away was bad enough. But after twenty minutes and still no sign of him, her heart plunged to her feet.

There could be several reasons why he hadn't arrived yet. While she claimed her luggage, she told herself not to panic. By now Nicky had started to fuss. She knew how he felt. After a search she found a bank of chairs and sat down so she could draw him out of the carrier to comfort him.

"Señora Di Rocche?"

Di Rocche—

Julie's head jerked up to find a Hispanic man in a sport coat and trousers addressing her. He wore a tag identifying him with the airline that had flown her down here. Why would Massimo have misrepresented their relationship to him?

"Y-yes?"

"Your husband had a problem that prevented him from making his flight here. If you'll come with me, I'll drive you to the hangar where a small plane will fly you to him in Raxruja."

She received the news with a combination of ecstasy and agony. "Thank you for coming."

"He told me to look for a beautiful American woman and a baby, both with hair as golden as the sun." The man smiled. "You were not difficult to find."

Massimo had made that remark about her hair before. If that was code to let her know this man could be trusted, she got it.

With his help carrying her bags, she followed him to a car parked outside the terminal. In a few minutes she and Nicky were delivered to a hangar on the other side of the airport where a one-engine plane stood on the tarmac in the early afternoon sun.

She swallowed hard, never having flown in anything that small. But she couldn't complain now. Six weeks ago she'd told Massimo she would live with him in the jungle if it meant she could be with Nicky. Now was the time to prove it.

The middle-aged pilot ran around to help her and Nicky inside the four-seater. With little fanfare except to fasten them in, they were airborne. When her heart regained its normal beat, she looked out on the amazing scenery below.

Beyond the city she saw rolling hills of the highlands. Every so often the green carpet yielded a clearing full of Mayan ruins. Whole civilizations of people had once lived here. Centuries later their cities were overgrown with vegetation just waiting for someone to come along and unearth their secrets.

For the first time she gained an inkling of understanding as to why Massimo was so fascinated.

Nicky had no idea what lay beneath them. Neither did she, really. A sense of unreality pervaded her world. The only thing that mattered right now was to reach Massimo. Then she'd be able to breathe again.

In a few minutes the pilot made a signal with his hand. The next thing she knew they were descending. Out of the window she spied a tiny air strip. Saying a little prayer, she closed her eyes and waited to feel the ground beneath them.

The landing turned out to be less bumpy than she would

have imagined. The plane came to a stop on a dime. When she opened her eyes again, she saw Massimo striding swiftly toward them.

He'd dressed in khakis and boots. When his jet-black eyes flashed her a private greeting, her heart flew to her throat.

She undid her seat belt, then Nicky's, but she was trembling so hard again she was all thumbs. He threw open the passenger door. Even with a tormented expression marring his handsome features, she thought him the most marvelous sight on earth.

Out of the corner of her eye she saw two strong, sun-bronzed arms reach for the carrier.

"Niccolino—" He lifted him in the air the way he did after his bath, then kissed his tummy.

Nicky made such happy noises, Massimo could be in no doubt his nephew recognized him. The low, joyous male laughter she'd waited for reached her ears. It was a wonderful sound that would stay with her forever.

Endeavoring to keep her composure, she moved rather than flew to the doorway where Massimo waited for her. With Nicky nestled against his right shoulder, he used his left arm to reach for her.

In the next instant he'd crushed her against his side. "Forgive me for not being at the airport," he whispered into her hair. "It was unavoidable." The feel of his breath sent spirals of delight through her body.

"I believe you, and it's all right. You warned me to expect the unexpected. I've been christened," she answered shakily.

"You're a brave liar." He kissed the side of her neck before lowering her to the ground. The friction created by their bodies left her breathless.

The pilot had already placed her bags next to the baby carrier. He observed the scenario with a smile. "The little one has your wife's hair and your eyes. You are a lucky man, *señor*."

Massimo subjected her to an intimate perusal. "You have no idea," he murmured. "Shall we go? After we get to the boat, it's only a twenty-minute drive downriver, then you'll be home."

Home.

Being here brought him alive in a completely different way. She found his energy had infected her, and pressed a hand to her throat.

He ushered her and Nicky to a van parked a short distance from the strip. Once everything was packed inside, he drove them to a tiny settlement.

"Welcome to Raxruja. As you can see, it's little more than a few streets, but it has the only accommodations for miles around."

He pointed out an army base straggled around a bridge. "This is the Rio Escondido, a tributary of the Pasion." Farther downriver from the bridge she saw a boat that looked as if it could hold about ten people. The only occupant appeared to be the male driver.

Massimo made the introductions. "Carlos? Meet my wife, Julie, and our son, Niccolo."

She shot Massimo a questioning glance, but he acted as if he hadn't noticed and helped her inside.

"Congratulations on your marriage, *señora*."

"Thank you," she mumbled.

"When Massimo went away, no one expected him to return a married man. You have a fine son."

"I think so, too," Massimo answered for her. With a half

smile he stepped into the boat carrying Nicky. The first thing he did was put him in an infant life preserver.

"Carlos runs this concession for the tourists visiting the ruins," he explained. "Today he helped me out because the motor on the other boat died halfway here."

"I see." She smiled at the other man. "I'm glad you came to his rescue. Nicky and I weren't too happy when he wasn't at the airport in Guatemala City."

"These things happen. You grow used to them."

"So I'm learning."

Massimo trapped her gaze as he handed her an adult life preserver. "My wife is a trouper."

The other man grinned. "She would have to be to have married you. I envy you more than you know."

Julie looked away. She needed an explanation, but had to go along with Massimo until they were alone. Their relationship had to be based on trust or it would never work.

Carlos started the motor. Soon the boat headed to open water.

"Your first trip into the jungle has begun," Massimo said in a mysterious aside. He held the baby close to him. "What do you think of it, Nicky?"

Julie knew what *she* thought.

The green canopy he'd told her about was thick and dark and alive, just as he'd said. An atmosphere totally foreign to anything she'd experienced in her life. She didn't know if she liked it or not.

There was only one reason she was here. That reason was sitting across from her. A magnificent man who'd aroused a frightening passion in her.

Deeper and deeper they penetrated the eerie green. You'd never know a human was anywhere around. Then her attention was caught by a small group of huts, each surrounded by dense vegetation. Massimo had fixed up one of them to be their living quarters.

Carlos steered the boat around a bend where she saw a compound of tents half exposed in the foliage.

Imagining it had been one thing. Seeing it, smelling it, feeling it was something else again.

She sensed Massimo's eyes on her. When she looked at him, she detected a glint of something akin to fear. But that couldn't be right. He wasn't afraid of anything. It had to be a trick of light.

A man and a woman emerged from a path beneath the trees. They walked toward the boat. The short, slightly balding male wearing glasses looked to be in his forties. In contrast the woman was maybe five years younger.

Julie noticed at once she was a tall, striking brunette with hair fashioned in a braid that fell to her waist and swayed as she moved. Her brown eyes fastened hungrily on Massimo.

Julie felt a dagger stab her heart. This was the woman in Guatemala Massimo had left behind.

He stood up with Nicky. Turning to Julie he said, "I'd like you to meet Dr. Scott Reese who's in charge of this dig. Dr. Gillian Pittman is his assistant. Please meet my wife, Julie, and our son, Nicky."

The woman named Gillian slowly eyed her and Nicky without pleasure. "How do you do." She spoke the queen's English in a chilly tone.

The other man gave her a warm smile. "Welcome to Cancuen, *señora*." He was a friendly American, thank goodness.

"Please. Call me Julie."

"I answer to Scott. I'm sure you and the baby are exhausted. You'll need time to acclimatize. Massimo's been working around the clock to get things ready for you. Go ahead and settle in. You'll meet the rest of the group at dinner."

"Thank you."

Dr. Pittman put her hands in her back pockets. "I don't have to tell you this is no place for a baby."

Massimo's jaw hardened. "If Nicky doesn't adapt, we have an alternative plan. Now if you'll excuse us, I haven't seen my wife for three weeks."

"Lucky you," Scott muttered before walking away.

Julie's cheeks stayed hot all the way along the path as she followed Massimo to their hut nestled in the undergrowth.

"What do you think?" he asked minutes later, after she'd had time to give it a thorough inspection.

She was too overwhelmed to talk. For a place in the jungle, it was utterly fabulous.

"Julie?" he said her name urgently.

Her eyes sought his. "You've made a real home for us here. After what you told me about Cancuen, I didn't think it was possible."

His chest heaved visibly. "The hut comes with a generator."

"And a high chair and a crib." He'd already given Nicky a bottle and had laid him inside it. "What more could a person ask for."

One black brow lifted. "But—"

She rubbed her palms nervously against the khaki material covering her hips. "I don't understand why you've told everyone we're married."

He held on to the back of one of the wooden chairs placed at the dining table. "Why do you think?"

The question flustered her. "I…I don't know."

"Scott was eating you alive. Carlos salivated the moment

he saw you. The pilot's probably in cardiac arrest right now. But for one couple with a two-year-old, the rest of the group is made up of red-blooded men. It's a miracle Jose delivered you to the plane."

"That's absurd. There are plenty of gorgeous women everywhere. I saw lots of them at the airport."

"They don't look like you," he murmured.

She shook her head. "If my brother were here he'd say Gillian Pittman was a knockout."

He moved closer to her. "I avoided Gillian from the beginning. Does that answer that question?"

Massimo didn't lie. His explanation about the other woman was more than satisfactory.

"What's the real reason?" she asked in a tremulous voice.

He folded his powerful arms. "That was a small part of the real reason."

"And the big part?" By now her heart was pounding so hard she felt suffocated by it.

"Have you forgotten who my role model was?" His voice rasped.

She had to think a minute before it dawned on her. "You mean your father…"

"That's right. The *uncle* who made visits to my mother on the isola whenever he could because she refused to marry him. I'm no different than he was when it comes to having my heart's desire."

Her heart leaped. "Massimo—"

"Fortunately for him there weren't any other men on the island to threaten their joy in each other. I had no choice but to stake my claim in advance, so be warned, Julie Marchant. I'm willing to wait for you.

"I beg you not to make me wait too long, though, to make

you my bride. We never know when fate will step in to change things. But for their accident, my father probably would have won my mother around to the idea."

Her eyes filmed over. "What an idiot I've been."

He shook his dark head. "No. Your willingness to put my happiness before yours is the kind of gift a man dreams about. I'm in love with you, Julie."

She ran to his arms, needing to show him. All she could do was cover his face with kisses. "I don't remember a moment when I wasn't in love with you," she cried. "I've missed you so desperately these past three weeks."

"Tell me about it," he said before his mouth descended and they began kissing each other senseless. It was joy incomprehensible not to have to hold back.

"I'll marry you anytime you say, darling," she said sometime later.

"I've already made the arrangements with the local priest in Flores for tomorrow," he admitted.

"That soon?" she blurted, so happy she was soaring.

"I still have the paperwork from the last marriage that didn't take place. Besides, your father left me with some final words. 'Make an honest woman of her to please her old dad.'"

"He didn't—"

His low chuckle thrilled her. "I promised him. It will make our wedding night something to cherish."

"It's going to kill me, but I agree." She cupped his face in her hands, loving him so much she couldn't stand it. "Do you think we could formally adopt Nicky soon?"

A tender smile broke out on his striking face. "I'm way ahead of you. After his bout with rosiola I considered him our first-born."

"So did I," she whispered.

With their arms around each other they walked over to the crib. Nicky always lay with his arms outspread and his little fists clenched.

"Massimo? Do you suppose—"

"Do I suppose Shawn and Pietra had this in mind when they drew up the will?" he said. He could always read her thoughts.

She bit her lip. "Of course they couldn't have known what was going to happen."

He looked down at her through eyes that burned with desire. His hands smoothed the gold silk away from her temples. "Whether they had a premonition or not, whether they'd died or not, you and I would have eventually met and found our way to each other."

"I believe that, too."

Massimo kissed her eyes and nose. "I didn't entertain thoughts of marriage until I came out here for the first time. After a hard day's work, I would return to my tent and imagine what it would be like to have the right woman waiting for me. The same woman in my bed every night. The mother of my children."

His hands slid to her arms and tightened. "I feared it would always be a fantasy. Then I met you. Do you have any idea how terrified I was when you walked in here a little while ago? I don't think I could have handled it if you didn't want to stay."

The fear she'd glimpsed earlier was no longer a mystery.

"I'd have stayed no matter what. You're my life, Massimo. Humor me and let me show you."

HARLEQUIN

More Than Words

"I have never felt more needed as a physician…"

—**Dr. Ricki Robinson,** real-life heroine

*Dr. Ricki Robinson is a Harlequin More Than Words
award winner and an* **Autism Speaks** *volunteer.*

SUPPORTING CAUSES OF CONCERN TO WOMEN

HARLEQUIN

WWW.HARLEQUINMORETHANWORDS.COM

MTW07ROBI

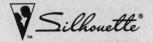

Romantic
SUSPENSE

**Sparked by Danger,
Fueled by Passion.**

The Taken

Tierney Doyle is used to being criticized for
her psychic abilities, yet the tough-as-nails—
and drop-dead-gorgeous—detective has no doubt
about what she has uncovered in the case of a
string of unsolved murders. And Tierney is slowly
discovering that working so close to her partner,
detective Wade Callahan, could be lethal.

Look for

Danger Signals
by Kathleen Creighton

Available in April wherever books are sold.

REQUEST YOUR FREE BOOKS!
2 FREE NOVELS PLUS 2
FREE GIFTS!

HARLEQUIN ROMANCE®

From the Heart, For the Heart

YES! Please send me 2 FREE Harlequin Romance® novels and my 2 FREE gifts. After receiving them, if I don't wish to receive any more books, I can return the shipping statement marked "cancel." If I don't cancel, I will receive 4 brand-new novels every month and be billed just $3.57 per book in the U.S., or $4.05 per book in Canada, plus 25¢ shipping and handling per book and applicable taxes, if any*. That's a savings of over 15% off the cover price! I understand that accepting the 2 free books and gifts places me under no obligation to buy anything. I can always return a shipment and cancel at any time. Even if I never buy another book from Harlequin, the two free books and gifts are mine to keep forever.

114 HDN EEV7   314 HDN EEWK

Name _____ (PLEASE PRINT) _____

Address _____ Apt. _____

City _____ State/Prov. _____ Zip/Postal Code _____

Signature (if under 18, a parent or guardian must sign)

Mail to the **Harlequin Reader Service®:**
IN U.S.A.: P.O. Box 1867, Buffalo, NY 14240-1867
IN CANADA: P.O. Box 609, Fort Erie, Ontario L2A 5X3

Not valid to current Harlequin Romance subscribers.

Want to try two free books from another line?
Call 1-800-873-8635 or visit www.morefreebooks.com.

* Terms and prices subject to change without notice. NY residents add applicable sales tax. Canadian residents will be charged applicable provincial taxes and GST. This offer is limited to one order per household. All orders subject to approval. Credit or debit balances in a customer's account(s) may be offset by any other outstanding balance owed by or to the customer. Please allow 4 to 6 weeks for delivery.

Your Privacy: Harlequin is committed to protecting your privacy. Our Privacy Policy is available online at www.eHarlequin.com or upon request from the Reader Service. From time to time we make our lists of customers available to reputable firms who may have a product or service of interest to you. If you would prefer we not share your name and address, please check here. ☐

SILHOUETTE

SPECIAL EDITION™

Introducing a brand-new miniseries

Men of Mercy Medical

Gabe Thorne moved to Las Vegas to open a
new branch of his booming construction
business—and escape from a recent tragedy.
But when his teenage sister showed up pregnant
on his doorstep, he really had his hands full.
Luckily, in turning to Dr. Rebecca Hamilton for
the medical care his sister needed, he found
a cure for himself....

Starting with

THE MILLIONAIRE
AND THE M.D.

by *TERESA SOUTHWICK,*

available in April wherever books are sold.

HARLEQUIN *Romance*

Coming Next Month

Spring is in the air this month with brides, babies and single dads, and the start of two new can't-miss series: *The Wedding Planners* and *A Bride for All Seasons*.

#4015 WEDDING BELLS AT WANDERING CREEK RANCH
Patricia Thayer
Western Weddings
Dark, brooding detective Jack allows no one to get close—until he takes on stunning Willow's case. His head tells him to run a mile, but will he listen to his heart instead?

#4016 THE BRIDE'S BABY **Liz Fielding**
A Bride for All Seasons
Events manager Sylvie Smith has been roped into pretending to be a bride for a wedding fair—but she's five months pregnant, and the father doesn't know yet! Then she comes face-to-face with him...and his eyes are firmly fixed on her bump.

#4017 SWEETHEART LOST AND FOUND **Shirley Jump**
The Wedding Planners
The first book of the sparkling series in which six women who plan perfect weddings find their own happy endings. Florist Callie made a mistake years ago and let a good man go. Now she keeps her heart safe. But the good man is back, and Callie might just get a second chance!

#4018 EXPECTING A MIRACLE **Jackie Braun**
Baby on Board
Pregnant and alone, Lauren moves to the perfect place for her soon-to-be family of two. Then she's blindsided by her anything-but-maternal attraction to her sexy new landlord, Gavin!

#4019 THE SINGLE DAD'S PATCHWORK FAMILY **Claire Baxter**
Being a single parent is hard, especially when there's been heartache in the past. Chase had planned to raise his daughter alone. But then he meets single mum Regan, and the pieces start falling together again.

#4020 THE LONER'S GUARDED HEART **Michelle Douglas**
Heart to Heart
Josie's longed-for holiday is in a cabin in an isolated Australian idyll. Her only neighbor for miles is the gorgeous but taciturn Kent Black, who has cut himself off from the world. And Josie can't help but be intrigued....

HRCNM0308